THE

UNDAUNTED

BOOK FOUR OF THE RED JAVELIN SERIES

ROSS HARRINGWAY

THE UNDAUNTED

COPYRIGHT © 2016 Ross Harringway

OMEGA PRESS

An imprint of Omega Communications Group, Inc.

For information contact:

Omega Press
5823 N. Mesa, #839
El Paso, Texas 79912

FIRST EDITION

Printed in the United States of America

OTHER BOOKS BY ROSS HARRINGWAY

FROM OMEGA PRESS

The Clovis Legacy Series
The Forbidden Region

Reign of Death

Shadows in the Dark

Weakness is Provocative

Illusion of Freedom

Burdened with Morality

The Red Javelin Chronicles
Red Javelin

Shroud of Cleopatra

Doctrine of Avoidance

Editor's note:

Some of the events in this novel occur simultaneously with the novels Red Javelin and Shroud of Cleopatra.

CHAPTER ONE

To say he had been born with a silver spoon in his mouth was an understatement. Osric Jenssen had led a life of luxury and ease. He was a great grandson of the Glorious Leader and was given access to unlimited money, space craft, women and leisure time. Osric was just shy of his ninety-fifth birthday when he was murdered. He had lived on Space Station Cy-5, which was at the edge of the Akarzdamedian Solar System. It was a military outpost for the most part, but there were hundreds of merchants that made their living on that station selling goods for long space travel. The Space Station had several five star hotels, food and clothing stores, areas to requisition fully charged solar cells and dunkle materie filters and many self-employed engineers and mechanics to repair space craft that happened to dock with the station.

Osric was not a merchant, nor an engineer. He simply existed in his fully furnished three floor apartment near one of the vast food courts of the station. Osric was mostly metal and not man. His skeleton had been replaced piece by piece over the last few decades with metal implants. His eyes were no longer his own, but new robotic eyes which enabled him to see better and farther than he ever had before. Osric was tall, well-groomed, and handsome and dressed in the best linens and satins. He normally looked as if he were going to a toga party. He rarely was alone as he had many high priced prostitutes that he could choose from to bed whenever he desired. He cared little for the race of the women or men that he took to his bed, nor did he care about their age. The youngest he had slept with had been an eight year old orphan boy with a cute smile. The boy did everything Osric asked of him and was paid well for his services. The morality of the transaction mattered little to Osric. All that mattered to him was that his physical needs had been satisfied.

He received a monthly stipend from the Royal Family in return for his simply sending reports as to the political scene on the station. Osric and his offspring would carouse the station, befriend many space travelers, obtain incriminating statements from those travelers and then turn them over to the authorities for execution. Osric's reward was his handsome stipend and the right to keep all of the property owned by the traveler that espoused any treasonous language. It was often that Osric and his children would make up accusations against travelers just so they could obtain their space craft. After all, who would dare accuse a member of the Royal Family of lying?

Osric and his many children thought that they had it made in that multi-level space station that was two AU away from the nearest populated moon. They acted with impunity and took all that they wished. They were above the law.

When Osric was killed, he had just learned that there was a rebellion that had broken out on several planets in the Eight Solar Systems which challenged the control by his family. He soon learned that several of his children and grandchildren had been found in their equally plush apartments dead. Each of them had their throats ripped open and were left to bleed out on their floors. Osric asked one of his grandchildren, an officer on the space station, to investigate the murders.

Osric was not the first Jenssen to die on Space Station Cy-5 that week. Osric had several illegitimate children that lived on the Station that were still alive the day he was killed. His last act as a Royal Family member was to urge his offspring to flee the space station and find refuge on Sikorsky's Planet. Some took his advice, packed their belongings and left on some space craft that they had stolen from some innocent traveler that they had betrayed. Some stayed. Osric died wishing he had heeded his own advice.

After meeting with his last few surviving children, Osric dined at his favorite food court location, called "Soshanna's," and enjoyed a large plate of Chicken Jerusalem with a bottle of dry white wine and a salad. He took an hour to finish his meal before walking back toward his lovely apartment. He overheard the space station news service announce that the Second Fleet had initiated a blockade around Sikorsky's Planet and that due to that insurrection martial law had been mandated for Cy-5.

Osric decided that he would be best served by locking himself in his apartment until things returned to normal. He arrived safely to his apartment and disrobed, as he preferred to live naked. He verbally instructed his apartment computer system to display a three dimensional broadcast of the top ten universal news stories as he walked toward his large kitchen. On his left was a well-stocked wine closet. He found a bottle of 2301 Chenin Blanc from Old Earth and opened it. He poured himself a full goblet and walked slowly toward his rectangle shaped red leather couches so that he could relax while taking in the current events.

But he was not alone.

Hiding in the hallway leading toward his back bedrooms was a Kotek, a half feline and half human hybrid with dark blue fur. She was just over five feet tall standing upright. She was double jointed as were all of her furry counterparts. She had claws just like a predator cat would and sharp fangs as well. Her long tail moved slowly as she waited for the right time to strike. Her senses for smell included that ability to sense fear in her prey. Osric was not afraid at all which meant he was unaware of her presence. Her name was Blu Bauslaugh, a prominent member of a travelling acrobat family. She left the family business to assist the growing rebel factions. Her orders from the rebel leader on the space station were simple: kill as many Royal Family members as you can.

Osric took a large gulp of wine just before Blu pounced on him from behind. She landed on the back of the couch, and perched herself over his head. She slashed his throat with her sharp claws extended on her fingertips of both of her hands. Osric futilely grasped at his neck as his life blood spilled all over his chest, couch and marble tiled floor. He rolled to the floor, gasping as he attempted to focus on his killer. He died within thirty seconds of the attack.

Blu calmly used Osric's master bedroom shower to cleanse herself of any blood. After she had showered, she ransacked his apartment to make it look like a robbery gone wrong. She dressed in a one piece black and burgundy outfit with maroon knee high boots. She had a black back-pack which she filled with all of the jewelry she could find in Osric's apartment. Her rebellion commander would be able to utilize the jewels to purchase illegal weapons. She was not worried about security cameras or DNA evidence. The cameras had been disabled a week before her planned assassination of Osric.

She was met at the doorway by her friend, Amy Ortiz, who cleansed the apartment with the latest air spray that annihilated any and all DNA evidence in an enclosed area. Amy had dark hair that was tied off into a ponytail and wore an unassuming outfit consisting of a loose fitting green tunic, brown pants and dark brown leather boots. She wore no jewelry or makeup in an effort to avoid calling attention to herself.

"Any problems?" Amy Ortiz asked softly as she sprayed down the room where Osric's body laid.

"None," Blu smiled, showing her fangs.

"Good. We just got a tip that a real VIP is arriving on the station. If we can recruit him to our cause, it would be an enormous PR victory."

Blu licked her lips, "Who is it?"

Amy smiled at her, "One of the heroes of the Blood Moon Incident. He will be docking soon. We need to be ready to get him away from the MI soldiers. You up for it?"

Blu nodded. "Sure. Which of the Blood Moon heroes is it?"

"Les Gillis."

Blu smiled, "The one that made the speech? I remember him. He was really handsome. I'm in heat right now, so getting him to join us would be my pleasure."

Amy laughed, "He is married."

"His wife can watch us breed," Blu laughed. "Or she can join in. Hell, I really don't care."

"Do you think he would be willing to join us?"

Blu nodded, "I think he would fight for the right cause. So yes. Yes. He will join us."

Amy continued spraying down the apartment and looked over at Osric's corpse. "Damn, Blu. You really messed him up. Glad you and your family are on my side."

Blu let out a meow, "The only good Royal is a dead one. I'll get it done any way necessary."

CHAPTER TWO

It had been a long flight with many transfers and sleepless nights. Lester Brey Gillis felt his adrenaline level rising as the private transport ship Captain announced that they would be docking with Space Station Cy-5 within the hour. Gillis had felt fortunate in that he had not been recognized by any of the other passengers as one of the participants in the Blood Moon Incident. Normally Gillis would be hounded by autograph seekers or business men or women that hoped to enter into contractual agreements for Gillis to endorse a product or two. Gillis had agreed a few times to have his likeness used to help some corporation to sell some service or product to civilians. Gillis had been well compensated for those transactions and was able to pay for nicer clothes, more guitars, and more expensive jewelry and designer clothing for his wife, Sophia. Additionally, Gillis was able to pay for his round trip flight from Sikorsky's Planet to Space Station Cy-5 without wiping out his savings. He was also able to fund the expenses for his wife to fly from planet New Edinburgh to the space station so they could enjoy a week together.

Gillis had found the six day flight to the station relaxing. He had been able to read news on his hand held computer. There were numerous blogs and private web postings that indicated a civil war was brewing between the Glorious Leader and some unknown factions. Gillis read that his own mother had been giving speeches in Ireland advocating seceding from the United Nations form of government and out from under the two hundred year rule of Secretary General Sikorsky. Due to the outspoken nature of his mother's advocacy and his own short lived fame from the Blood Moon Incident, Gillis attempted to maintain a low profile. His mother had advocated cessation, which the mention of was an act of treason. Gillis walked around the large transport ship, keeping his head down to avoid eye contact with any of the other passengers. He acted as if he cared little for the observation windows that made it possible for the passengers to look out upon the beauty of outer space. The floors were carpeted with light blues and greens to muffle the sounds of boots and shoes on the metallic floors. He made it to one of the large observation decks and looked out at outer space, admiring the stars.

The idea of a war terrified Gillis. He had studied military history and the lessons he learned were that wars brought destruction and death. Rarely did the wars finish the feud. Many warring factions would fight again, sometimes over several generations. Although the people of Earth had been involved in many wars in the two hundred year rule of the Glorious Leader, humanity had won them all. The death toll for humans had been light in comparison with the alien planets that were conquered. If a revolution were to occur, the body count could be astronomical. The Glorious Leader had proven to be very good at one thing: killing. Gillis leaned against the observation window, staring at the space station in the distance as he contemplated the uncertain future that the current war might bring.

Space Station Cy-5 had been designed and built three decades earlier. It was massive, able to house over fifteen thousand humans with ease. The interior of the space station had a state of the art engineering section that kept the station rotating clockwise to slowly simulate the rotation of a planet. The station also maintained numerous oxygen regeneration machines so that the military presence and civilians could breathe clean air. There would also be numerous soldiers working in the weapons areas to protect the station from attack by pirates or alien invaders. Gillis also knew that there would be a "Tank," which was the holding cells for anyone that broke the laws or just got into trouble for public intoxication or some other infraction. The station would have about eight hundred military service men and women, mostly Military Intelligence, Marines, Weapons officers and some pilots. The rest of the military would be in engineering, computer science, criminal investigation division or medical positions. Cy-5 was primarily used as a stopover between solar systems, so that space travelers could rest, purchase fully charged solar cells or fuel, acquire additional provisions, change ships or to trade foods and services of money or other goods.

Gillis smiled as he watched the grey and black structure as his transport ship grew closer. The station had a cone shape in the center that was painted black. Connected to the center cone were eight connection bridges to four metallic wheel designs. The four wheels were parallel to one another and each one had a different purpose. The wheel at the bottom of the station was the enclosed docking area for small one or two man ships to park as well as Raumschiffs and Super Raumschiffs. In the docking area there would be security officers to check identities of the passengers of the ships and space craft serial numbers. Once a ship landed on the platform, it would be rotated by machinery into an airtight holding area, decontaminated, scanned and then cleared for entry into the main docking area. Once the ship passed through the procedure, it would be moved into the main hangar which was large enough to comfortably house several dozen Raumschiff sized space craft.

For the larger space craft, like the transport ship that Gillis was currently a passenger, the space station would lower what was known as the "Docking Extensions" which were metallic arms that were similar to walkways that would connect with the space craft to allow the passengers to leave the ship and walk onto the space station.

There were several miles worth of "Solar Collectors"

facing the sun that was several astronomical units distance from the space station. The Solar Collectors were each about a kilometer long and wide and would store the energy from the sun into large power batteries. Once the batteries were full of solar power, the Solar Collector would jettison the power battery to the space station. The batteries would be either used to keep the space station operational or would be sold to private transport ships or given to United Nations Battle Cruisers.

"You're Les Gillis, aren't you?" A female voice asked from Gillis' rear.

Gillis slowly turned to see two Kotek's standing behind him. The one that had spoken was a female with black fur on her back, the top of her head and the majority of her arms and legs. Her feet, neck and chest were covered with white fur. The bottom of her cat shaped face was also white. She had brilliant green cat's eyes. Her pointed ears were black, her whiskers white. She was about five feet six inches tall. The second Kotek was a male, solid black with yellow eyes and about six feet tall.

"Yes," Gillis admitted to them. No sense in denying it. He had been fortunate on this trip; these were the first two civilians to approach him. Either his longer hair and dress down look had fooled everyone else, or others were intimidated by his commercials and willingness to fight as he had on the Blood Moon. "I am Gillis."

The two Kotek's smiled, revealing sharp fangs.

"I told you," the female Kotek said to the make, her long

black tail was twisting left and right. "What brings you, a universal hero, to a transport ship like this?"

"I am on vacation," Gillis told them. "I am at a disadvantage, you know who I am. But I don't know you. What are your names?"

"My name is Cris Jeanna Bauslaugh, but everyone calls me CJ." The female introduced herself, extending her hand that seemed to be part human, part cat. Gillis shook her hand. "And this is my twin brother, I mean he is not identical, but we were from the same litter. His name is B.B. Bauslaugh."

Gillis shook the hand of B.B, "What does 'B.B.' stand for?"

"I like to run into things," B.B. said, meowing at the end of the sentence. "Not on purpose. I am just sometimes clumsy. So the B.B. is for 'Broken Bones' or "Bam Bam' or 'Bad Boy.' Take your pick."

"Nice to meet you both," Gillis smiled. Although there were several of the human-feline hybrids on Old Earth and at his Academy, he had never been up close to one before. This was certainly a new experience for Gillis. He noted how their hands felt different than a one hundred percent human hand felt when he had shaken them. The cat-human hybrids had claws and short fur that was soft to the touch. He was certain he had heard of the name Bauslaugh before. "So, what brings you two here?" He pointed out the observation window toward the approaching space station.

"We are meeting family," C.J. purred. "We have never met a famous person before."

"Some of my classmates at the Academy were feline-human hybrids, but I have never met an entire family before," Gillis responded as he watched their long tails wag. "What line of work are you two in?"

"We are entertainers," C.J. smiled revealing a row of sharp fangs in her mouth. "We do acrobatic acts for the most part. We travel with a group from the Nevada High Flying, Death Defying, and The Amazing Gymnasts."

Gillis smiled at them both. He had heard of their company on the news reports. They would travel from ship to ship, planet to planet to entertain the troops and civilian populations. They were well known and tickets to their performances were expensive. "Well, then I am the one that has met some famous people today. I would love to see your performances sometime."

"Give us your computer address and we can electronically mail you our schedule." B.B. suggested.

Gillis told them his electronic mail address as the captain of the transport ship announced that they would dock with Space Station Cy-5 within ten minutes. They shook hands again as Gillis told them they should return to their assigned seats for the docking procedures.

Gillis moved through the crowd of passengers on the transport ship. He felt the craft shake a few times which caused

Gillis to stumble into the hallway wall. He noticed that a few other passengers fell to the red carpeted floor. He heard a loud set of banging noises on the hull of the ship. Gillis immediately knew what it was; the transport ship was under attack. The banging noises were from laser fire impacting the metallic hull.

Gillis felt his heart pounding in his chest as he ran back toward the observation deck. Other passengers were screaming and running in panic. Gillis pushed through them as many of the passengers were running in the opposite direction, directly toward him and blocking his path. Gillis heard the warnings from the ship's Captain for everyone to return to their seats and secure their safety harnesses. Gillis was having none of that, he wanted to see for himself what was going on out in space.

Gillis pushed through the crowd as the other passengers were rushing the opposite direction. He noticed a couple of individuals preaching calm. They had the sign of the cross tattooed on their faces, just as Gillis' deceased friend Porfirio Cardenas had. Gillis made his way past the crowds and looked out into space through the transparent metal observation area. There were dozens of small one man fighter ships, Allen Corporation Fighter Type CC76A3 space ships, engaged in a space battle. Some ships were chasing others, firing laser bursts at them. Other ships were flying in from the north to join the melee. Gillis instinctively stepped backwards as a ship erupted in an explosion after it had been strafed by several laser bursts. Whoever the pilot had been had not stood a chance. The numerous space craft speeding in from the north began to assist one of the sides in the battle, firing upon several ships. Gillis observed several more space craft erupt in explosions. Pieces of metal were flying off in different directions, some of the metal shards impacted on the hull of the transport.

Gillis looked off in the distance at Space Station Cy-5. The forty-seven level floating station was also involved in the battle. The weapons crews on the Space Station were firing rockets and lasers at one of the factions of space ships. Gillis watched as several smaller ships were blown up. He deduced that this was far more than a normal raid from space pirates. This seemed to be an all-out war. Gillis, as a man with an inquiring mind, wanted to know what was happening.

The Captain of the transport ship announced that they would be docking with the space station within five minutes. Gillis ran for his seat, pulling out his hand held communication computer device. "Computer, download all broadcasts coming from and to Space Station Cy-5 in the past ten minutes. Analyze the reports for the attacks occurring out in space."

His computer responded quickly, "There was an attack by a rogue squadron which was repelled by Space Command fighter ships. All of their rogue space craft were destroyed."

"How many?" Gillis asked.

"Thirty-two ships attacked the space station. All were destroyed in the battle."

Gillis rounded the corner of the hallway toward the

passenger seating area. "Who were the attackers?"

"Not enough information to respond," his computer answered. "But their ships were Allen Corporation fighters and I have analyzed their serial numbers. They each were from the military base on lunar settlement Robert Andrews."

Gillis found his seat and settled in as the transport ship began to decrease speed for a safe dock with the space station. The moon that had been named Robert Andrews was about two astronomical units distance from Space Station Cy-5. The moon had been terra-formed several thousand years ago and was named after one of the heroes of the past wars. Robert Andrews had been one of the leaders that defeated the Akardamedians over two hundred years ago. The Akarzdamedians had named the moon "Zheviatovo," which meant "outpost" in old Earth English.

Gillis heard docking clamps from the space craft connecting with those of the station. Anxiously desiring to exit the transport ship, the passengers began standing up as the ship came to a halt. Gillis stood and began to move toward one of the several exits that would lead to the lower level of the space station. Clearly there were events in play that he had to investigate. Although Gillis desperately wanted to spend a week of romance with his wife Sophia, he did not want her, or his friends traveling with her, to end up in harm's way.

Gillis waited for the protective hull of the transport ship to slide open. He followed the crowds out of the ship and onto the fifty foot long walkway to the space station. He heard another explosion, which caused many of the civilians in the walkway with him to scream in terror. If the hallway was breached, all of them would be swept out into outer space and be dead. The crowd began to run in panic for the lobby of the space station. Gillis ran also, not wanting to be trampled to death.

As he arrived at the large holding area of Cy-5, Gillis was not all that surprised to see that martial law had been imposed. There were men and women being forced into lines by camouflage fatigue garbed Marines and solid black uniformed Military Intelligence soldiers. Gillis watched in anger as a man was protesting just before the Military Intelligence Lieutenant in charge fired his laser rifle into the man's midriff. The poor man was blown in half. His legs hit the metal floor of the space station just seconds before what remained of his upper torso fell with a thud. He saw a half dozen other bodies of civilians on the docking bay floor. The burn marks around their wounds indicated that they had been cut down by laser fire. Gillis took note that each of the dead bodies had no offensive weapons on them. They had not been a threat to the security forces, but were killed nonetheless.

People were screaming in panic, others were weeping over the corpses of lost loved ones. Gillis walked slowly now, hoping to avoid calling attention to himself. He saw several other dead bodies strewn about the metal floor, all of them were wearing civilian clothing. A large family of Kotek's meeting C.J.

and B.B., the two he had met on his flight. They were hugging each other close; some were licking the other on the face. They were frightened by the looks in their cat's eyes and the way they kept looking over their shoulders. Several Marines were collecting the luggage from the transport ship that Gillis had arrived on. They were searching each piece of luggage using hand held computer scanners. Gillis walked past some of the dead bodies and studied them closely. Most of the corpses had the sign of the cross on their faces; others did not and seemed to be every day average citizens. The stench of burnt flesh permeated the area. Several of the passengers that had arrived with Gillis were covering their noses due to the foul smell.

Gillis knew the meaning of the sign of the cross well. His roommate at the Academy, Drayton Love-Easter, was the son of one of the most charismatic religious leaders in the entire Eight Solar Systems. Pastor Love-Easter encouraged his followers to tattoo their faces with the sign of the Cross of Jesus, to let the world know that they had accepted the Lord into their lives. Gillis wondered why the military would be killing the followers of Pastor Love-Easter. They were peaceful people and had a reputation for obeying the rule of law. They showed love to their fellow man through good deeds and charitable acts. Killing them served no purpose to the security of the eight solar systems.

But yet, they were being systematically executed by the soldiers on the space station.

Gillis moved into one of the lines so that he could be processed and get out of the docking area. He needed to get to his hotel room for privacy so he could contact his wife and warn her as to the events on the station. If there were any of the followers of Pastor Love-Easter on board Giles Lancer's ship, their lives could be in danger.

Gillis waited patiently as the lines moved slower than normally. Once he finally made it to the front of the line, Gillis was confronted by an officer in a black Military Intelligence Class C uniform and three enlisted Marines. The Marines had their laser rifles aimed at the line. The officer, a First Lieutenant whose name tag read "Jenssen" approached Gillis.

"Place your hand on the identification scanner," Jenssen ordered coldly. He was a tall and broad shouldered man with thick blonde hair and blue eyes. Gillis noted a cruelty in the eyes of the man. He seemed to take pleasure in murdering all of the Christians whose bodies littered the floor.

Gillis complied with Jenssen's demand by putting his right hand on the glass top of the table before him. A blue light under the glass passed back and forth, collecting data from Gillis' hand. A ten inch tall and twenty inch wide, three dimensional screen appeared before the soldiers, showing Gillis' picture with his complete resume, school grades, his weight, height and marital status. Jenssen read from his computer screen the complete analysis of Les Gillis.

"Lester Brey Gillis. I know who you are. What is your

business here on Space Station Cy-5?" Jenssen asked, glaring at him. He had seen the entire drama of the Blood Moon Incident unfold live, via computerized broadcast, as had the rest of humanity. Gillis had been the one to wire an underground train to detonate underneath the hide out of the Rosenburg killers. Gillis had also put together a defensive set of barricades to slow the attack of the Rosenburg family and their hired killers. Jenssen smiled slightly. The Rosenburg's were Jenssen's cousins. Revenge against Gillis would be sweet.

"Vacation sir," Gillis answered. He hoped not to be interrogated by the seemingly blood thirsty soldiers. Gillis decided he would be best served by keeping his answers short and not volunteer any information.

"Vacation?" Jenssen looked past Gillis and up and down the line of passengers behind him. Jenssen hoped that his friends, Yuri Gorski, Julia Steiner or Drew Harrison would be with him. Being able to kill them all at the same time would have brought a great feeling of elation to Jenssen. "Are you traveling alone?"

"Yes, sir."

"Well, there is much trouble here on the space station," Jenssen warned. "Several acts of treason have occurred here and Martial Law has been imposed. The soldiers on this station have been ordered to shoot to kill and suspected of espionage or treason. Understand?"

"Yes," Gillis affirmed. "Can I go?"

"No, you are not cleared." Jenssen pointed in the direction of the stacks of luggage and back packs that had been searched. "Collect your belongings and you will be escorted by me to the prison for processing."

"For what reason?" Gillis protested as two tall and muscular Marines approached him. One stood at Gillis' left, the other on his right. Each Marine grabbed a tight hold of his arms. He was surrounded and outnumbered and he had no chance of escape. He decided to not struggle at this point. He would wait for an opportunity to fight back.

Jenssen had drawn his laser pistol and aimed it at Gillis' chest. "You were one of the murderers on the Blood Moon Incident. Your mother in Ireland is encouraging rebellion against the Glorious Leader. She has given several dozen speeches in support of Irish secession from the United Nations. You helped kill several members of the Rosenburg clan. As you are certainly aware, they were all members of the Royal Family. You sir, are a traitor."

"I am nothing of the sort!" Gillis felt the two Marines shackling his wrists together with metal cuffs. "I demand a lawyer and to see the Magistrate. I know my rights."

"Rights are for the living," Jenssen whispered into Gillis' left ear. "You see, on the way to the Tank, you just might have an accident. Caine and David Rosenburg were my cousins. You really fucked up by taking a part in killing them."

Gillis smiled now, "You should have heard the way Caine cried when Julia stabbed him. He sounded like a nine year old girl, begging for her life."

Jenssen slapped Gillis across the face, his palm open. The Marines held Gillis upright as his head turned to the right under the impact.

"Is that the best you can do?" Gillis said as he regained his composure.

Jenssen slammed his fist into Gillis' abdomen and knocked the wind out of him. Gillis doubled over and groaned.

Gillis was forced to walk forward by the Marines. Jenssen was behind him, his laser pistol aimed at his back. Jenssen warned him if he tried to run, he would fire. Another Marine walked over to the luggage stacks and found Gillis' large back pack that was lying on the metal floor. The Marine threw it over his shoulder and walked rapidly toward the travel tubes with Jenssen and the two other Marines escorting Gillis. Gillis wanted to protest that they had left his guitar behind. If he made it as far as the tank he could entertain all of his fellow prisoners by playing them a few tunes.

Gillis walked with the men, taking in all of the sights and memorizing every detail. The hallways were metal and about twenty feet wide, connecting to metal walls that were eighteen feet high. The ceilings were metal as well, with small cameras to record all of the activity in the halls. No doubt the recordings would be broadcasted directly to the security section. Gillis was concerned, not for his own safety, but for Sophia's. Gillis had believed that surviving the Blood Moon Incident was a gift from whatever Gods were in control of the Universe. He was living on borrowed time. He and the other survivors were fortunate to have lived through the several attacks that they had endured.

Gillis estimated that the ship owned by Giles Lancer would arrive in about fifteen hours. Based on the situation, he needed to warn his wife and friends as quickly as possible. As Gillis was forced to walk rapidly down the metal corridor, he heard other soldiers talking about Pastor Love-Easter declaring the Glorious Leader to be an abomination against God. From what Gillis heard, the Pastor was advocating that the Royal Family should step down from power to allow humanity to create a new form of government. Based on his advocacy, the Glorious Leader declared Pastor Love-Easter and all of his follower's to be traitors. Vladimir Sikorsky had ordered that all of the followers of the Pastor to be killed on sight. The mark of the cross on those believers was now an excuse for the military to carry out death sentences against them.

Gillis arrived to an Elevation Tube that would get him to the third ring around the central cone of the space station and ultimately to the Tank. The entrance doors to the tube were dark red contrasting itself from the light grey color of the rest of the surrounding metal. There were six Marines now assisting

Jenssen. There were two Military Intelligence enlisted women dead on the floor, their throats had been ripped out and their blood was spattered all around. Gillis was stunned when he saw on the metal wall large capital letters that were written in fresh human blood. It said: "HAZ PATRIA! MATA UN SIKORSKY!" The blood had still not dried and was dripping onto the floor.

Gillis had learned to read and write Spanish in grade school. In his mind he translated to himself, "Be a patriot! Kill a Sikorsky!" It was all out war on the Royal Family, Gillis thought to himself. No wonder they wanted to arrest him. Gillis would be a good hostage to use against his rebellious mother.

The red Elevation Tube doors slid open. Gillis was pushed inside the tube by Jenssen and the Marines. Gillis saw no other passengers inside the white tube. There were two dozen light blue seats, which were empty, and some rail bars on the walls for extra people to hold onto while standing. Gillis walked in and stood at the rear red doors of the long tube. He looked down at the metal floor and noticed that there was blood dripping onto it. Gillis slowly moved his gaze upward without moving his head and looked up at the ceiling. He saw eight Kotek's hanging onto the ceiling by their claws, baring their fangs. There were five solid black furred feline-humans, a multi-colored one, a solid white Kotek with light blue eyes and the last one had black and white fur. The six Marines and Jenssen stood facing Gillis. Gillis quickly looked downward as he did not want to give his soon to be jailers any hint that there was potential danger above them.

The doors slid shut.

The eight cat people retracted their sharp claws and dropped from the ceiling onto the Marines and Jenssen. Gillis backed against the wall and watched as the furry attackers slashed the Marines to ribbons with their razor sharp claws. Most of the unfortunate Marines died with their throats ripped open, their blood spattering in every direction. Jenssen tried to run for the door, but a muscular black Kotek leaped onto his back and ripped out Jenssen's throat with his powerful fangs. Jenssen was dead before his body hit the floor.

The eight turned their attention to Gillis.

"Hi," Gillis swallowed. With his hands cuffed behind his back, Gillis was easy prey for the feline-human hybrids.

"Get the keys and release him," the larger black cat-human hybrid ordered. "Strip their uniforms and take their weapons."

Gillis felt relieved as the solid white cat person with the blue eyes removed the handcuffs.

"Thank you," Gillis said as he looked into the eyes of each of his rescuers. "I don't know how to repay you."

The large black one stood over Gillis, his muscles were rippling, his jaw dripping with Jenssen's blood. "I am Bauslaugh. My children call me Dracula. My children and grandchildren here are Midnight, Snowflake, Mittens, Wolvie, Summer, Blu and Stripes. We know who you are and so did these dead soldiers. Your actions on that Blood Moon have turned you into a target and celebrity at the same time. The speech you gave has inspired many to rebel against the Royal's. As you can see, we have no love for the Glorious Leader or his army. You wish to thank us for saving you? You will thank my family and me by joining the war against the Royal Family."

Gillis felt the hot breath of the one named Dracula on his face. Clearly the cat-human race did not understand concepts such as personal space. He was also intrigued by their names as they were similar to the names that humans would give to their pets to describe their fur colors or personalities. Gillis could feel the Elevation Tube moving upward. The computerized voice was counting off floor numbers.

Gillis shrugged, looking over the dead, nude soldiers bodies. The Kotek's were a race able to fight. All of the cat-human hybrids were watching Gillis as he pondered the offer to join them that came across as more of a demand. Gillis paused before answering. He recalled the Rosenburg family and their efforts to kill him and his friends on the Blood Moon, during the Blitzkrieg ambush and during the sand storm. Gillis had no love for the Glorious Leader or his descendants. But a rebellion was not the first goal in his mind. With a Raumschiff full of friends and his wife slated to arrive on the Space Station turned into a war zone, Gillis wanted to ensure that they either arrived safely or turned back to avoid the dangerous situation.

"Although I am grateful for what you all just did, by freeing me from these jerks, I will join you all on one condition."

"And what is that?" Dracula asked.

"That we save my wife and friends. I was going to meet them on this station for the holiday," Gillis explained. "They will be arriving here in a few hours. Can you help me? Is there some place safe that I can contact them from?"

Dracula looked over to another large, muscular black furred male with bright yellow eyes. "Midnight, take the point. We are going to take Mister Gillis to Dos Guero's Muertos."

Gillis was not surprised that the Kotek's knew his identity. He was certain that the feline-human hybrid's risked their lives to save him precisely because he was Les Gillis. Had he been some random tourist he would be cooling his heels in the Tank or suffered some fate even worse than that.

The one named Midnight growled and dropped down on all four legs, ready to spring when the doors opened. The white one named Snowflake did the same. Gillis was fascinated as he watched his rescuers double jointed legs and arms. They seemed to go from standing upright to walking on all fours without effort. Gillis rubbed his hands together apprehensively. A bar called Two Dead White Men did not bode well for a Caucasian of Celtic descent. Gillis hoped for his own sake that the Bar name was only a play on words and not a mission statement.

CHAPTER THREE

Cadet pilot Jack Harcourt was elated when Giles Lancer invited him to sit in the co-pilot's chair on the Blue's City. Harcourt had been spending the majority of the week long space flight to Space Station Cy-5 getting to know the young Andolini's on board, lifting weights and studying flight manuals. Ever since his roommate, Michel Darcel Evart, had graduated, Harcourt had become a loner. That is, with the exception of the occasional Gorski Gang gathering. As one of the leaders of the Gang, Harcourt did maintain close contact with Klaus Rhinehard and Jen Staszko regarding party planning and investigating new potential members. Other than those few moments, Harcourt buried himself in his studies.

Lancer had noticed that Harcourt seemed to be in need of a friend and invited the Child of Athena to help him fly the Super Raumschiff. Harcourt was wearing a purple turtle neck sweater and black cargo pants. Lancer was in a one piece brown flight suit. Harcourt took the seat next to the larger man and buckled the safety harness over his shoulders.

"Thanks for the invite," Harcourt smiled at Lancer.

"Thanks for the company," Lancer smiled back. His normal co-pilot, Elvis impersonator James Hill, was asleep in the lower level bunk beds. Lancer and Hill would alternate flying the ship when they would venture out into deep space. They would generally trade off twelve hour shifts. The *Blue's City* was safe to be left on computerized pilot, but Lancer preferred to have a live person sitting in the pilot's seat at all times, especially when they were transporting civilians as part of their cargo.

Harcourt stared out at the darkness of outer space before him through the transparent metallic windows of the pilot's section. There were many stars visible in the distance. "How much longer until we arrive at Cy-5?"

"About a day," Lancer pointed to the far left corner of the long computer dash board that went from wall to wall of the pilot's section. It was about thirty feet long and two feet deep. There were some monitor screens that displayed the rear and side views of the space craft as well as many control buttons, dials to gauge oxygen and fuel levels and many other mechanisms critical to fly the ship. Harcourt noticed Lancer was motioning to a timer that was programmed to count down the hour, minute and seconds of the flight time.

"That is useful," Harcourt began looking over the control panel. He noticed that one section had been redesigned from the original Super Raumschiff's. It was clearly a weapons panel. "Do you find much trouble in deep space?"

Lancer nodded, seeing where Harcourt's eyes were inspecting. "You would be surprised. There are space pirates that attack without warning. Plus, there are occasional rogue elements like civilians in distress that will try and hijack your ship. One cannot be too careful out here in this vast emptiness, all alone with no one to help you."

"I don't blame you," Harcourt had heard of the pirating in space. It was apparently a profitable scheme, to take another space ship by force, murder the inhabitants and then sell the ship on the black market.

"So, Jack, can I call you Jack?" Lancer picked up a bottle of whiskey that had been stored in a cooling unit beneath the control panel.

"Sure," Harcourt watched as Lancer poured a cold cup of whiskey and then a second. Lancer handed Harcourt one of the cups. Harcourt took a sip and coughed as the cold whiskey burned the inside of his throat as it went down. "That is damn good."

Lancer laughed, "From Old Earth, I get a case every time I take a load there. It is from an old brewery in Scotland that has been in business for about five hundred years. So, Jack, I have met many of your race, the Children of Athena. You seem different from the others. Why is that?"

Harcourt pondered the question put to him as he sipped some more of the whiskey. "I suppose because I have always been unwilling to use my special gifts, or powers as some call them. Other Children of Athena use their powers on humans without even contemplating the ethics or the morality of their actions. I refuse to do so. Think about it. How would you like to have your most private thoughts read by someone like me? Or, even worse, have your decisions altered or your behavior controlled. I know I would not like that happening to me so I don't do it to other people. There are some Children of Athena that view their powers as a means to an end. They use their powers to get things that they normally could not have. Normally they use subtle mind control to entice a person to sleep with them or do some other act."

"Like what that one did to Drayton Love-Easter?" Lancer took a drink. Since Lancer had spent most of his time flying cadets from Clovis Academy back and forth between Space Station Cy-7 and planet New Edinburgh, Lancer had gotten to know many of them. He had spent several hours conversing with Love-Easter, Gillis, DuBravac and Yesenia Guevara. Lancer had heard the tragic tale of how Melissa Harcourt used her pheromones and possibly her mind control powers to seduce Love-Easter.

Harcourt nodded, "Exactly. Melissa uses her powers to hurt others, and she did it to Dray and Yesenia. Broke them up. It was despicable. The rest of us, I mean the rest of the Children of Athena, we shun her, avoid her. People hate us enough and then she goes and makes it harder on the rest of us to find acceptance with normal humans."

"Do you and your other members of your race find yourselves the victims of racism?"

Harcourt drank the whiskey and savored the flavor as he considered the question. "Yes, there have been incidents of racism against us. That was how I got to know Yuri Gorski, Michel, Dray, Les, the Andolini brothers and Drew. Some asshole construction workers picked a fight with me. I fought as best I could, but I was beaten down, overwhelmed by the numbers. Gorski and his friends saved my life. Those guys intended to kill me but Yuri led his gang to my rescue. They brought me in without question and each one of them, over time, became my closest friends."

Lancer took a small swallow of his whiskey. "I have heard of such things on other planets. Children of Athena being murdered by gangs of humans. It is sad that even today there is still racism."

Harcourt looked down at his cup, "My father and mother told me that they were almost killed by a group of drunken military enlisted men, before I was born. I had an older sister that was murdered by a group of racists. They raped and killed her, for no reason. Just because she had skin as white as cotton. Just because she was different."

Lancer could hear the pain in Harcourt's voice. Losing a sibling had to be one of the most heart breaking events one could suffer. "I am sorry for your loss. I hope you do know that not all men and women are that cruel."

Harcourt nodded remembering Evart and the two years they had been roommates at the Academy. Evart had proven to be a trusted confidant. "My friends taught me that. The years I was Michel's roommate were good times. I miss him. I miss all of the Gang that have graduated. I hope they are all doing well in their careers. I have learned from them all, especially Yuri, that friends need to be loyal to one another, no matter what."

Lancer smiled and leaned over, holding his cup of whiskey up high. "Cheers to friends."

Harcourt tapped his cup to Lancer's, "Cheers to friends."

The two men took in a sip of the whiskey, smiling. Lancer was all right, Harcourt had concluded to himself.

Rolf Rhinehard had been watching for his opportunity to strike. He had spied upon a married man on board the space craft that had a two year old child. The man was named Joseph Bolt. He had eight wives that Rolf knew of. One of those wives was named Minxia Lu Bolt and she had caught Rolf's attention with her lovely face and athletic body. Joseph Bolt was an overweight computer programmer in his late fifties. Bolt never took care of his body. He ate bad foods and drank to excess. Minxia was in her early twenties, in great shape, vibrant and spent her spare time in the gymnasium on the bottom level of the *Blue's City*. Rolf always enjoyed a good work out and was able to watch Minxia for several days. She had great legs, a pretty face, flat stomach and nice buttocks. Rolf had been flirting with Minxia for several days now, hoping that the time would come when he could get her into his bed.

During the times Rolf interacted with Minxia, he had learned that the woman was not completely happy in her marriage. She had been very young and the wedding had been arranged by her family to the non-athletic Joseph Bolt. According to her, she had been given to Bolt at the age of sixteen to pay off a family debt. For Minxia, she had no choice but to marry the older man. It was a matter of family honor.

Over the days that they were in contact, Rolf concluded that Minxia was flirting back. She was ready for Rolf to take her. He had seduced many married women as well as women in committed relationships. He had learned how to read their signals, whether they were amenable to an affair. This woman was ready. Rolf caught her on several occasions eyeing his muscular physique with lust on her face. He was cognizant that their flight would end within one or two days, the estimated time that of arrival at Space Station Cy-5. If he was going to experience a sexual session with Minxia, he had to act quickly.

On that morning, Rolf found that Minxia was running on a treadmill in the small gym. She was wearing a half shirt, tight shorts and tennis shoes. They said good morning to each other. Rolf had on a sleeveless shirt and shorts. He sat down on a bench and began affixing round weights on metal bars to begin his work out. His bulging muscles rippling as he went about his business. He watched the woman out of the corner of his eye. She was watching him, smiling.

Rolf set down his weights and walked directly toward Minxia. He saw the glimmer in her eyes as he got close to her. He picked her up, his hands under her arms, and began kissing her passionately. She responded by kissing him back, running her hands over his muscular chest and shoulders. They undressed each other quickly and he pinned her against the wall of the gymnasium, near the entrance to the small showers. He kissed her all over her torso as she explored his body with her hands. He thrust his erection inside of her and smiled as he heard her moans of pleasure. After he finished making love to her against the wall, he carried into the showers and took her again, underneath the warm water of one of the stalls.

After they had finished, Minxia seemed embarrassed and made an excuse that she had to get back to her husband and his other wives. She rushed out of the showers and recovered her discarded clothing in the gym before leaving. Rolf dried off and decided to continue his work out. As he made his way to the gymnasium, he noticed that Sophia DuBravac was there. She had a twenty-five pound dumb bell in each hand, doing curls to work out her biceps. She saw that Rolf had joined her in the gym when he sat down at the bench press he had been at before he took care of his lust for Minxia.

DuBravac looked over to Rolf as she alternated her right and left arms, curling the weights up and down. "You know, Rolf, one day someone is going to kill you."

He laughed out loud. "So you saw her as she came out of the showers? I doubt her wimpy, fat husband would have the balls to try and take me on."

DuBravac lifted her right arm up and pointed the twenty-five pound dumb bell at Rolf. She had been waiting for the opportunity to give him a tongue lashing for his bad acts. "I'm not talking about Bolt. You screwed over Piotr! And what about Supreet? You didn't even invite her to come along with us on this trip. She was hurt. How could you do that to her? And now this woman? What is it with you and married women? One day you will mess with the wrong man and they will make you sorry."

"I doubt it. I am sorry about Piotr, but Mia Nguyen was not his girl. She was a free agent. Piotr was too young for her anyway. Sure she liked Piotr, but she never considered him her steady boyfriend. I feel like I did Piotr a favor. As for Supreet, we had established a while back that our relationship was a friends with benefits thing. We sleep together now and then, but it is not serious." Rolf picked up some dumb bells and began lifting them over his head to work his shoulders. "You see, Sophia, having sex with a married woman is less complicated. There's no commitment. I get what I want and they go back to their boring lives. I don't have to put up with some clingy woman bothering me all the time. I get to come and go as I please. I answer to no one."

DuBravac glared at Rolf. "You never want children? A family?"

He laughed at the thought of that. "I already have a child or two. I knocked up Dean Harvard's youngest wife two years ago. Harvard thinks it's his son. Why would I want to get tied down to that? Changing diapers, waking up at all hours of the night to feed a needy child. That is not my idea of living."

"You had an affair with one of Golden Harvard's wives?" DuBravac began laughing hysterically before she finished the question. "You risked getting expelled from the Academy for a piece of ass?"

"Yes, and she was worth it and she was not the only one. There was a Nurse at the hospital in Clovis City that is pregnant, most likely from me and not her husband." Rolf set down his weights. "So, I have spread my demon seed already. I don't need a ball and chain wife to procreate."

"Rolf, if you want sex with multiple women, you could just marry dozens of girls." DuBravac continued her curls. "You know the laws permit men to have as many wives as they wish. Why don't you just marry a few and you can avoid the danger of some jealous husband coming after you. Your brother married April and he is very happy."

"My brother is a fool," Rolf began selecting some heavier dumb bells. "He followed April Mejia around like a lap dog for over a year. All the while she was getting laid by men with less morals than me, if that's possible."

"Watch your mouth!" DuBravac warned, her voice rising with anger. "April is one of my closest friends!"

"So then you know what I say is true. April, knowing that my brother was enamored with her, would run off with any random fly boy for sex, leaving my big brother lonely. So now they are married and expecting parents. Big deal. She will burn my brother in a Frankfurt minute and you know it." Rolf found the weight he was searching for on the racks of dumb bells. "There are very few women that find one man and love only him. Look at you. When you met Les, you two were together and pretty much inseparable. There was Yesenia that loved Dray. Harumi and Dominic. Arch and Elektra. Women like you,

Yesenia, Elektra and Harumi are almost impossible to find."

"People change, Rolf. April changed. She realized that her past behavior was not in her best interests. That was why she reached out to your brother. She loves him more than you seem to give her credit for. Rolf, you are handsome, smart, a talented pilot and have a great career ahead of you. You should stop your self-destructive behavior before it gets you into big time trouble."

Rolf started lifting the heavier weights over his head. "So say you. I know what I am doing. I promise to be more careful, if that will make you feel better."

In the break room, on the next level up, there was a friendly game of poker going on. The game of the day was Texas Hold 'Em. In the corner of the break room was a round table that could seat up to eight people. The competitors at the table had each paid in thirty Old Earth Dollars to obtain thirty thousand chips. The players had all decided that the winner would take all of the money and the others would leave with nothing once they lost all of their chips.

Seated around the seats were cadet pilot Norman Porter, a freshman and new Gorski Gang member. Porter was a skinny white male, about six feet tall. He was eighteen years old with crooked teeth, dark hair and brown eyes. His parents never had the money to pay for a dentist to fix his teeth, thus Porter was self-conscious regarding his dental issues and rarely smiled because of it. He had been born and raised on a mining colony on planet Athena. His parents were emotionally supportive of the dreams he had to become a pilot and took out several loans to pay for his transportation to planet New Edinburgh.

Porter had been assigned to be the room mate of Lucius Andolini, who was sitting to his right. Lucius was following in the footsteps of older brother Marco and studying to become a pilot. The younger Andolini boy had the same handsome looks of Marco and Dominic. He was the same height and his build was similar to his older siblings. Even his hair and eyes were the same as his older brothers'. Lucius had been born with four other siblings. His parents had been taking sanctioned drugs to stimulate pregnancy and produced a large family. Lucius had enjoyed his childhood with all of his numerous siblings. Just as Marco and Dominic had been, Lucius was an exemplary soccer player and had joined the Clovis City professional futbol team to earn extra money while he attended the Academy.

Sitting to Lucius' right was his twin sister, Venus. She was a beautiful young girl of eighteen years old, dark hair, light brown eyes, curvaceous body and a smile that would cause any man to turn their head her way. Venus was also studying to become a pilot. She had followed older brother Marco around over the years, learning how to play cards and how to spot an opponent trying to bluff her. Venus knew that using her good looks, especially in a poker game, was too her advantage. She had on a light green tube top that exposed plenty of cleavage and brown shorts. She had played in card tournaments many times, but her opponents would almost always find her body distracting.

Venus was sitting next to the other Andolini on the flight, Giola. She and Venus were difficult to tell apart, almost exact twins. Giola was studying to become a weapons officer, just like her older brother Dominic. Giola was louder than Venus and generally the more vocal of the two. Giola was a bit more modest in her clothing, wearing a one piece, light blue, and sleeveless old flight uniform that she had bought at a trade market on planet New Edinburgh. The uniform had a gold zipper line that went from her navel to her neck, which she normally kept zipped all the way up. But, on their way to play poker, her sister Venus had pulled the zipper down enough to expose Giola's cleavage. When Giola protested, Venus explained to her that it was an advantage to use her body to distract the male players.

Seated next to Giola was cadet freshman Daniel Choi, a weapons major. His family was originally from Korea on Old Earth. His previous two generations had traveled to other planets in search of work and fortune. Choi had left planet Cootron to become a cadet at Clovis Academy. He had dark hair that was long due to his love of heavy metal music. Choi was a Gorski Gang member due to his defense of Giola when she was attacked by some of the Bragg Gang earlier in the semester. Choi had put Xavier Bragg in the hospital and sent the others running. Choi was honored to join the gang as he had watched Yuri Gorski and the others on the live broadcasts of the Blood Moon Incident. The fact that Gillis' wife Sophia and Jurgen Doerntz were on the same ship with him was cause for Choi to find every dollar he could scrape together to pay his part for the trip.

The sixth and seventh seats were occupied by Doernitz and Lila Zapata. The young married couple were juniors at the Clovis Academy. Doernitz had been one of the survivors of the Blood Moon Incident. His wife, Lila, was an engineering student. Both were earning excellent grades and enjoyed reading technical manuals and attending lectures on the most up to date discoveries. The last seat was taken by a large burly man named Wellington Choksey Harriak. His friends called him W.C. He had below the shoulders curly brown hair, a bushy beard, a large stomach from too much beer and ale. He was almost seven feet tall with broad shoulders. Harriak was a retired miner from planet Cootron. He was in his sixties and had some scars on his face and arms from years of accidents in the iron mines. He had suffered several broken ribs, broke his left arm four times and his right twice. He had been married several times and widowed each time. His children were all grown and each had gone their separate ways in the vastness of space. His children never came back to visit him as he had been physically abusive with them over the years. Harriak believed his treatment of his children was for their own good. Now, he was a man alone, living out his final years touring the solar systems to alleviate his boredom.

Venus had the largest stack of chips. She had just won a big hand off of Doernitz who now had only eight hundred dollars in chips left. Harriak was the dealer of the next hand. Doernitz looked at his two down cards. He had the ten of clubs and the ten of diamonds. Doernitz pushed his remaining chips in the middle of the table.

Giola was surprised to see her two down cards were two Aces. She tried to hide her joy, as Venus and Marco had taught her, but she could not. "All in!" She was laughing with joy. She noticed that her sister Venus gave her a dirty look. Everyone else quickly folded their hands. Unfortunately for Doernitz, the Aces held up and he was the first at the table to be eliminated.

"Good hand," Doernitz said as he stood up from the table. He looked at his wife Lila. "I am going to get a drink, can I get you one?"

Lila nodded, "Thank you baby. Apple Juice?"

"Be right back," Doernitz told her as the next hand was being dealt.

Doernitz walked over to the bar that was in the same room and picked up two cups of apple juice. He walked back to the poker table and gave one to his wife.

All of the participants of the poker game turned their heads when they heard Lancer clearing his throat. The other civilians that were in the break room that were not a part of the poker contest also stopped talking. Lancer's face looked grim. His eyes looked over each of the passengers, as if he were sizing them all up.

"Who died?" Harriak asked when he saw the expression on Lancer's face.

"I thought you should all know," Lancer began, "that a rebellion has broken out. I just received news reports that the Martian Colonies have declared independence. Ireland and the

Nevada Territory on Earth have also made a similar claim. The governing council on Robert Andrews moon also voted to secede from the United Nations. The Sikorsky's have sent in the military to all of those areas. Battles are occurring as we speak."

"What does that mean for us?" Choi asked, breaking the uncomfortable silence.

Lancer shrugged, "Nothing as of yet. But if we do stay on course for Cy-5, we might not find it as hospitable as we had hoped. There might be enough of a following there to support insurrection, which would mean that each and every one of us would have to take sides. Also, the Robert Andrews moon is fairly close to the station. The cessationists on that moon might determine that the station has some strategic value and attempt to take it over. This could go very badly."

"We should contact my brothers," Venus spoke up. "They would know what to do. Especially Dominic, he is in MI."

"You have a brother in MI?" Harriak asked with suspicion in his voice. "They are all Narcs. They cannot be trusted."

Giola glared at Harriak, "My family can be trusted."

Lancer, sensing that an argument was about to start, deduced he needed to redirect the conversation. "Look, we are about half a day or so away from Cy-5. I will let each of you know if I receive any news from them. If you were planning on meeting friends or family at that space station, I suggest each of you attempt to make contact with them. Maybe they can give us some useful information as to what is going on over there."

Lancer left the break room as each of the passengers began doing as he had suggested. The Andolini kids immediately forgot the game of poker and were trying to contact their siblings on their hand held communication devices. Choi and Palmer were attempting to contact their parents.

Harriak crossed his arms, glaring at everyone. He wanted to complete the card game. In addition, there was no one that he could think of to contact. His children wanted nothing from him. His wives were all dead and his friends had been left behind after he retired. Harriak spent the time on the *Blue's City* enjoying the view of Venus and Giola. They would have been good wives, he thought. Both girls were attractive and had pleasant personalities. To be forty years younger, Harriak thought to himself.

Jurgen and Lila comforted one another, hugging each other closely.

"We should contact your sister," Lila suggested.

"I agree and your family as well," Jurgen kept hugging her. "I love you girl."

"I live you too, Jurgey." She smiled as she looked into his eyes.

Lancer left the room as he had other passengers that he was compelled to inform. He found Joseph Bolt, his eight wives and one son in the ship's restaurant. Lancer broke the news to them quickly. The wives seemed oblivious to the implications of a civil war. Joseph Bolt, on the other hand scowled at the news. The man had a huge payday coming his way at Space Station

Cy-5, and he was not about to allow a silly civil insurrection to ruin his business dealings.

CHAPTER FOUR

Dos Gueros Muertos was a large chain of bars that had nineteen locations throughout the eight solar systems of the United Nations of Earth. The majority of the bars were located on planets and lunar installations. There were only two located on space stations. The chain was owned by the famous Ortiz family from Honduras, Earth. They had taken four generations to grow the business to its' current success. They slowly opened new businesses, avoiding the mistake of rushing into a new market just to have a presence. The Ortiz business was savvier than that.   They would conduct marketing research for all potential new locations. They would examine the per capita income of the population. They would assess the military presence, the safety level, the cost to have certain goods imported to their new location. They would leave little to chance.

After conducting their business analysis of Cy-5 the Ortiz family determined that one of their bar locations would do well financially there. They opened Dos Gueros Muertos seven years earlier and had better than average sales there. They could pay the bills, the rents, inventory, employees, overhead and had a good profit at the end of the month to add to the family fortune.

Joseph Ortiz was the great great grandson of the original owner of the very first Dos Gueros Muertos. Ortiz was in his fifties and had moved to the Station after the family made the business decision to open the location there. Ortiz had a degree in business management, a master's degree in computer programming and a doctorate in marketing. He traveled to Cy-5 with his three wives and eighteen children. He had one son and the rest were daughters. His oldest child was thirty and his youngest was sixteen.

Gillis silently accompanied his Kotek rescuers to the large bar. He observed the fiesta colored sign of "Dos Gueros Muertos" as he followed the group of part human and part feline rebels. They dragged behind them the bodies of the dead MI and Marines they had killed in the previous battle. Gillis' calculated the events that had occurred before his eyes and the little information he had been exposed to and concluded that the civil war was expanding in scope. He had to contact his wife, Sophia, and warn her. In addition, Gillis wanted to contact his mother in Ireland to find out what her role in the current events had been.

The solid black furred Kotek named Dracula led the troop to the bar entrance and walked in through the sliding glass doors. The other solid black Kotek named Luna was right behind him. Gillis walked in third. The bar was like any other Gillis had seen. It had numerous tables, chairs, three bars with stools around them and viewing screens for the patrons. Gillis noticed that there were numerous people and Kotek's in the bar, drinking beers from mugs with the bar logo adorned on them. There were human waitresses, all brunette's and all attractive, serving the customers that were present. Gillis saw several of the customers had the mark of the Cross of Jesus on their faces. Others were injured; some with medical wraps on their arms, some their heads. One woman had a medical wrap around her hands.

At one of the round tables, Gillis noted that the seven people sitting around it were all individuals that had been in the news recently. Each one of the seven were wanted for treason. Gillis recognized them as they were overweight and had shaved heads. Even the women at the table had shaved their heads. He could not remember their names, only that the seven had killed General Ivana Feklisov of Sikorsky's Planet and escaped. Feklisov had been a daughter of the Glorious Leader and her murder led to an obscene money offer to bring back the seven perpetrators dead or alive. Gillis smiled to himself that the seven had been able to get this far with such a high bounty on their heads. Clearly they were a resourceful lot.

Gillis realized that the bar had been turned into a refuge for wanted criminals. As he walked around the bar he moved toward the center. He watched as the cat people began tossing the dead onto a pile of other dead soldiers. Gillis marveled at the pile of dead MI officers in the middle of the floor of the bar. He estimated there were about twenty dead.

As Gillis walked around taking in the scenery he noticed that everyone in the bar was watching him. Some had the look of awe on their faces. Others were pointing at Gillis and whispering to the person sitting next to them. Gillis saw an attractive brunette with olive colored skin smiling at him from behind one of the bars.

Gillis approached her and smiled back, "Please tell me you serve Harps beer."

"Yes we do, Les Gillis," the woman turned around and reached into a cooler behind her and pulled out a bottle of the beer he had asked for. She popped off the bottle cap and handed it to him. She watched as Gillis took a drink.

"Thanks. How much do I owe you?" Gillis asked.

"You owe us nothing, Les Gillis!" a man bellowed from one of the tables as he stood up to his feet. He was in his fifties, with dark hair with streaks of grey, short in stature and overweight. He pushed his chair away and walked toward Gillis. "You are Les Gillis, are you not? The hero on the Blood Moon? You wired the underground train to detonate under a safe house full of Sikorsky loyalists. You created the maze of death around your safe house that caused the deaths of many more Sikorsky servants. That was you? Yes?"

Gillis saw that all eyes were on him. He took another drink from the ice cold Harps beer. "I was not a hero and all the things you just spoke of, I had many that helped me. Drew Harrison, Julia Steiner, Yuri Gorski, Alan Anderson and the list could go on ad nauseam. All I did was decide that I was going to fight like the banshee himself to stay alive and get home to my Sophia. But to answer your first question, yes. I am Les Gillis."

The overweight man walked to Gillis and extended his hand. "It is an honor to meet the father of the Revolution. My name is Joe Ortiz. My family owns this bar and I am the leader of the resistance on this space station."

Gillis shook his hand, "Pleasure to meet you, sir. But I am not father to anything."

The rest of the customers in the bar stood up and one by one introduced themselves to Gillis. Most shook his hand. Some hugged him. During the Blood Moon Incident, Gillis had given a speech just before he detonated a train full of explosives underneath the headquarters of the enemy. Gillis had been told by many that his speech had been inspirational to them. That his words about fighting until your last breath had hit a nerve in the vast human population. When the greetings were done, Gillis realized that there was silence in the bar. They were staring at him in expectation of something profound, waiting for Gillis to speak. He took a drink of his beer and sighed. Speech time.

"I am honored to meet each and every one of you," Gillis began. "I am grateful to Dracula and his family for saving my life. I will forever be in your debt. I am not up to date on current events but from what I can tell there is a war going on, over what I do not know. My wish is that some of you can enlighten me as to the reasons for the conflict. If it is a fight for the fundamental liberties of freedom of speech, freedom of religion, freedom to love and to be loved, freedom to elect your leaders and freedom to pursue happiness then I would join that fight today."

Gillis was stopped by the thunderous applause from the audience. One of the women with the Cross tattooed on her left cheek ran to Gillis and hugged him, weeping. "May God bless you, young man!"

The woman was pulled back by another man.

"Please continue," Joe Ortiz encouraged Gillis.

"What you all saw when I was on the Moon orbiting Semiramis was a group of people with good hearts and a will to live come together." Gillis told them. "We were not heroes. We were just men and women like each of you present here today. On that moon, we had been ambushed and lost a good friend. Another was injured badly. With only eight of us left, we made the fundamental decision to stand together and fight to the end. My dear friends and I went days without sleep and prepared our defense. And when the time was right, we hit them back and we hit them hard. It was a miracle that we survived. We arrived on that moon with ten cadets. Two of our team died fighting for their lives and for ours. You called me a hero. I am not. Porfirio Cardenas and Pierre Zerbe were the heroes. And my life has been enriched by the fact that they were both my friends. I miss them every day."

"We do fight for freedom, Les Gillis." Ortiz stood again. "We fight for the values that you have advocated for. And we do so for many reasons. Your speech that you gave on the Blood Moon inspired us all. That is why we call you the Father of the Revolution. Your words, your example that you set for us all and your undaunted defiance against all odds. Les

Gillis, this rebellion needs you. We need you. We need you to lead us."

"We are not soldiers in the conventional sense," Dracula chimed in. "We need your knowledge of tactics to take this space station."

Gillis saw again that all eyes were on him. He was about to speak when a black and white colored Kotek pounced next to him. The Kotek had a fuzzy white and pink ball in his mouth and dropped it to Gillis' feet.

"That is one of my sons," Midnight told Gillis. "His name is Mittens for his white paws. He is only a few years old so he likes to play still. He wants you to throw his ball for him. I think he likes you."

The one called Mittens was purring and rubbing his face on Gillis' leg. Gillis reached down and scratched Mittens behind his ears. Only a few years old and Mittens was already fully grown. It seemed the physiology of the feline-human hybrids was something of a mystery to Gillis. He had never studied them. Gillis picked up the pink and white ball and threw it across the bar. Mittens immediately gave chase and pounced on the ball, looking at the siblings from his litter as if to challenge them to try and take the ball away from him.

Gillis began walking around the others. Other than the seven assassins of General Feklisov, there was no military experience in the lot of them. The cat people had speed, stealth and agility which would work well in a combat situation. But the humans were a rag tag group with no experience at all. Gillis was afraid they were all preparing for a suicide mission. He observed that each of them had a fire in their eyes that reflected a willingness to lay down their lives for the cause of freedom. They were each filled with a belief that this rebellion was the single most important event of their short lives.

"Okay," Gillis began. "I will help you. But first I have to contact my wife. I have to warn her to stay away from this station due to the dangerous situation. Does anyone here have any knowledge of life supports systems and engineering?"

An attractive Hispanic brunette wearing the uniform of a waitress raised her hand. "I do."

"Who are you?" Gillis asked her.

"Amy Ortiz, I am his daughter." She pointed to Joe Ortiz. "One of his many daughters. I studied engineering in college."

"Good," Gillis motioned for her to approach. "Anyone else with experience in engineering?"

Several Kotek's began to stand, including the playful one named Mittens.

"You have each worked on engine systems?" Gillis realized there was more to the feline-human's than he had realized. "Tell me your names."

There was a solid white Kotek with blue eyes named Snowflake. A multicolored cat with a bushy tail and eyes like a raccoon named Nappy which was short for Napoleon. A few with solid black fur were standing named Luna, Velvet, Panther, Corina, Jelly-Belly, Odysseus, Wolvie and Obsidian.

"Okay, you all come up," Gillis motioned for them to stand with Amy Ortiz. "If you desire to take this space station you must control the engine room and the life support area. We can shut off the Security and weapons sections and even the Command Station from there. I am certain the engine room is heavily guarded. It will not be easy."

"We are ready to fight," Luna said bravely.

"I am certain of that," Gillis looked to the others that were sitting in their chairs. "Other than the confiscated weapons from the dead soldiers, do we have anything else we can use to fight with? Knives? Weapons of any kind?"

Joe Ortiz and some of his daughters stood up and pointed to the door that had the words "EMPLOYEES ONLY" painted on it.

"Follow me," one of the Ortiz women said. She was wearing the uniform of a Marine Corps Sergeant that was blood stained. "We have plenty of weapons to choose from."

Gillis followed the attractive Ortiz woman and her father into the back storage rooms of the bar. "And your name is?"

"Karla," the woman answered as she led Gillis down several winding hallways, passing a large mechanical dish washer, several laundry machines, some storage rooms and finally to a larger office with five six foot by four foot tables. All of the tables were covered with weapons from ancient Earth. Gillis was taken aback by what he observed. Scimitars, katanas, samurai swords, morning stars, throwing knives, Thompson machine guns, two M-60 machine guns, several M-79 Grenade launchers and a few cases of grenades, three RPKS-74 sniper rifles, several 9 mm. Walther's, several 9 mm Uzi machine guns, stacks of clips of ammunition, ammo boxes, bayonet's and other various weapons from wars of several hundred years in the past.

"These are collectors' items. Each of these weapons is worth a small fortune to collectors." Gillis observed. "Karla, where did you get these?"

"A gun trader brings them in occasionally. My father and I like old weaponry so I would spend my money to buy a few here and there. Plus the guy is a pig and hopes to bed me some day so I lead him on to get a discount off of his price."

Joe Ortiz laughed at that. "She is amazing is she not, Les Gillis? She is not married and needs a husband. Perhaps you two should get to know each other better. Karla would make an excellent wife for you."

Gillis shook his head, "Well, my wife Sophia would probably not take it well if I brought in a sister wife to our lives. As much as I appreciate the sentiment, I would have to decline your generous offer."

Karla slapped Gillis on his rear. "Ask your wife. I know I would not mind being wife number two. I would bear healthy children for you."

Gillis rubbed his chin and shook his head again. "I have no doubt. I have a few single friends that would love to breed with a woman as beautiful as you. When this is all over, I will certainly hook you up. Now, back to business. The folks out in your bar, do they know how to use any of these?"

"No, I was hoping you could teach them." Joe Ortiz motioned over the tables with his hands. "It's not easy to practice with contraband weaponry with the Narcs always watching."

Gillis picked up a samurai sword and held the hilt in his left hand. He began swinging it around to get a feel for the four foot long blade. It felt perfect, aerodynamic and easy to handle. Gillis found the protective scabbard for the blade and threw it over his shoulder and tightened the sash around his waist. "This is a good blade. I could use it in battle."

"You studied the arts," Karla recalled watching Gillis in his fight to the death against the man named Chin on the Blood Moon. "So does this mean you can help show us how to use these weapons?"

"I can help," Gillis said picking up one of the Uzi's and pulled out the clip of 9 mm bullets. "When was the last time these weapons were cleaned?"

"They have to be cleaned?" Joe Ortiz asked innocently.

Gillis nodded to the two of them. They were certainly going to need training in all areas of using these types of weapons. Gillis worried that the little army Joe Ortiz had assembled would not be up to the challenge. Gillis began breaking down the Uzi in his hands. He checked the parts for rust or signs of age that might cause the weapon to misfire or not work properly. "You have any linseed oil?"

"Any what?" Karla asked.

Gillis hid his frustration at her response and changed the

subject. "Where can I make a contact, a secure contact, with an incoming space craft?"

"This way, Les Gillis." Joe Ortiz led him to another room.

Gillis followed them, "I need the two of you to think something over for me. This space station is a metal can that can be crushed. Taking her over is only half the risk. We are vulnerable to outside forces and attack. May I suggest that you confer with the others about another plan?"

"What did you have in mind?" Karla inquired.

"Escape," Gillis said simply. "I advise that we all get the hell off this station as soon as possible. After I talk with my wife, I will hear your answer then. But to take the station, we will lose most of your supporters out there. They are not soldiers and would be mowed down by the trained Marines and MI soldiers out on the station. Your rebellion would be over before it began. If we take out the offensive weapons systems and then flee on several Raumschiff's we can find a more defensible position in another location. Robert Andrews Moon might be an example of such a strategic base. Think it over."

Karla walked around Gillis and studied his face. "You speak of escape when you were the one that gave the speech to fight. That is out of character for the man I have spent hours studying. I know everything about you. You are not a man that runs from a challenge."

Gillis nodded in agreement, "Normally you would be correct in saying that about me. But starting a war on a space station is very risky. If an explosion causes a hull breach, well, that could make for a very bad day. Being swept out into space is a horrible way to die. So, Karla, why would you spend so much time studying me?"

Karla looked at her father and he shrugged at her. She looked back at Gillis and sighed. "Because you and your friends killed my husband on the Blood Moon. "I was one of the many wives of David Rosenburg. I had been kidnaped and was a slave until David decided he wanted me around for his own pleasure. When Colonel Gorski raided the Rosenburg Ranch and you and your friends killed David that gave me the opportunity I needed to escape. I owe my life to you and your friends. That is why I spent so much time learning about you."

Gillis had enjoyed the financial rewards of his popularity since the end of the Blood Moon battle. He had never really considered the impact his team mates had on others. Based on what Karla Ortiz was saying, they had touched many lives in a positive manner. But in the back of his mind, Gillis felt a bit uncomfortable with Karla. He had helped kill her husband. Even though she was expressing gratitude for the act, David Rosenburg had been her husband. Gillis began to doubt how much he could really trust the Ortiz family. Gillis had briefly met the woman named Dulce that had escaped similar circumstances from one of the Ragnarsson assassins. He determined to do as he had been taught by his mother, trust but verify.

As Gillis was contemplating the revelation given to him, Karla continued to speak about how she had been tortured as a hostage and forced into the marriage. Gillis was uncertain if the story was true or a concoction to build sympathy. She explained that she had been on a vacation with her parents at the age of twelve when she was taken from the space transport ship called the Esperanza. Karla never saw the faces of her abductors and only recalls waking up in what she later learned was Rosenburg's Ranch. She was forced to become a laborer and whipped when she faltered to do as ordered. As she grew older, Karla became friends with a girl named Juliana Rosenburg and the two were inseparable. When Karla turned seventeen, she was forced to marry David Rosenburg. She recounted the many events of family violence between her and her husband. She had been slapped, hit and beaten by him several times.

Then the Blood Moon Incident happened and her husband left her alone on planet New Edinburgh. She recalled Colonel Nikolai Gorski arriving with his platoons of Marines to arrest the criminals. During that time, Karla took a chance and fled for safety. She was able to secure a small space craft, fly to Lynott's Land and obtain assistance in contacting her family. She was soon reunited with her family. She repeatedly thanked Gillis for killing David.

Gillis listened to her as he was looking over the computer displays of the space station blue prints. He planned on offering no comments about her ordeal until she asked a cryptic question.

"When all of the Rosenburg's on the Blood Moon died, were they decapitated first?"

Gillis turned away from his monitors and raised his eyebrows. "Why would that matter?"

Ortiz looked down at the floor and then back into his eyes. "Because all of the Royal Family have a computerized microchip in their brains. When they die, all of their memories and experiences are uploaded to a satellite. Then the satellite transfers all of those memories to a dormant clone of the deceased and that clone is activated."

"Define activated."

"The clone is brought to life with all of the memories and experiences of the original. But if you decapitate them the nerve function to the brain doesn't activate the microchip."

"And the duplicate, or clone, never receives the uploaded data," Gillis concluded.

"Correct. That is why you must decapitate them. So did you? Did you cut off their heads before they died?"

Gillis tried hard to recall the events and the order in which the Rosenburg Team had died. He recalled that some were burned alive. Many shot with lasers. Others shot down while in their small space craft. But none of them had been decapitated. "No. None of them. Alfred was burned alive by one of my trip wire traps. Your husband was killed by a flame dart. Caine was stabbed to death."

Ortiz looked down at the ground again and then looked back at Gillis. "Then all three of them are alive again, somewhere. And David is extremely vengeful. Who killed him?"

"You didn't watch the live broadcast of the battle?"

"I did. I just don't recall the names of everyone."

"My friend Drew was the one that stabbed him with the flame dart," Gillis recalled. "Your husband had a body of reinforced bone structure. He beat the crap out of us."

"That was because he had died twice before. You see, the clones of the Royal Family are actually better than the original human body. They all have added abilities. Some have the metallic bones, others weaponry under their skin. They are extremely hard to defeat."

Gillis nodded, "Yeah, I remember. Any idea where the clones of David and Caine might be located?"

"Sikorsky's Planet," Karla said quickly. "I was told everything was located there."

Gillis felt a lump in his throat. Julia Steiner, Angelique LeClair and others involved were on Sikorsky's Planet. He had to warn them. "And how long does the process take, I mean to transfer their minds into the new host body?"

Karla looked down at her feet and fidgeted her feet. "It takes a few weeks unless done on the location where the Replicant is located."

"And how long does it take if it is done on sight?"

"Instantaneous."

"So you are telling me that Caine and David are probably running around somewhere on Sikorsky's Planet?"

"That is exactly what I am telling you," Karla said softly.

Gillis tapped his finger tips on the table in front of him for a few seconds. If Karla was correct then all of his friends were in danger. "If you will excuse me, Karla, I need to make some satellite connections."

CHAPTER FIVE

The conversation with her husband was short and to the point. Sophia DuBravac turned off her personal hand-sized computer-cam after she heard him tell her how much he loved her. Gillis was clear to her that Giles Lancer had no choice but to turn the *Blues City* around and return to planet New Edinburgh. Space Station Cy-5 was no longer a safe place to be. Listening in on her conversation with Gillis had been her friend, Lila Zapata.

"Wow, Sophia, what are we going to do?" Lila asked in her usual excited tone.

"We are going to do exactly what my husband said. Let's go find Lancer and tell him we have to turn around." DuBravac stood up and Lila dutifully followed her. They went from the lower level living areas to the steps leading to the second floor and the command area. They found Lancer there entertaining many of the other passengers with stories of his exploits in the military. Lancer was an amazing story teller and had an ability of captivating an audience with tales of past battles on other worlds.

Seated in the chairs were the eight wives of Joseph Bolt, Harriak, and a young couple that were named Curtis and Jill Mayne, Rolf Rhinehard and Lancer's co-pilot, James Hill. They noticed DuBravac and Lila walk in.

"Well, two of the hottest married women around have joined us," Joseph Bolt said of DuBravac and Lila as if he meant to insult all eight of his wives. Minxia Bolt looked longingly at Rolf, her stare indicating she would much prefer being with the cadet pilot as opposed to her pig of a husband.

"Giles, we need to talk. It is an emergency." DuBravac said, ignoring Bolt.

"What is going on?" Lancer asked her.

"My husband and I just had a conversation. He is on the space station right now. He told me that there is a serious problem over there. There is a rebellion going on board the station. There are quarantines in which people are being executed for no reason. They tried to arrest my husband but he was rescued. We have to turn the ship around and go home."

Lancer looked DuBravac in the eyes. She was certainly one of the toughest women he had ever met. Gillis was a truthful kid, if he said there was a reason to stay away from the station, then his word was gold with Lancer.

He looked up the ladder leading to the pilot section. The three Andolini, Lucius, Venus and Giola were up there watching the controls for him and Hill as they entertained the others.

"Hey!" Lancer called up to them. "Lucius! Have you learned how to bring a Raumschiff to a full stop?"

"Yes, Mister Lancer!" Lucius yelled back. "Why?"

"Do it," Lancer ordered. "Full stop."

Lucius scowled and looked at his twin sisters. They were all three wearing matching red sweaters and black cargo shorts. The girls enjoyed dressing the same as no one could really tell them apart. Giola and Venus were equally confused by Lancer's command, but watched in silence as Lucius began to program into the ship computer the command to bring the ship to a halt.

Joseph Bolt glared at the others as he was not happy with the decision to stop the ship. He had a business deal to conclude on the space station. He could not be delayed, regardless of the circumstances. "I think this girl is being hysterical. I paid really good money for you to take me and my eight wives to Cy-5 and I demand you get us there pursuant to our contractual agreement."

Lancer shot a look at Bolt. "Sir, I am responsible for the safety of each and every one of my passengers. That means you and your wives. And 'this girl' as you refer to her is married to a man that is one tough hombre. He survived the Blood Moon Incident. If Gillis says that the station is not safe, then that is good enough for me. I will not place people at risk and there was a clause in our contract that outlines this sort of thing, Mister Bolt."

DuBravac nodded and was glad they had chosen Lancer as their pilot. He was a man of common sense and had always been good to the cadets at the Academy.

Bolt shook his head and then reached under his shirt and

pulled out a hand laser in his right hand. With his left arm he grabbed the long blonde hair of Jill Mayne and yanked her toward him. He pinned Jill Mayne against his body and aimed the laser at her head. Bolt's wives cried out in disbelief. Jill Mayne screamed, her eyes wide open with terror. Her husband, Curtis tried to charge Joseph Bolt, yelling for him to release his wife.

Joseph Bolt aimed his laser at Curtis Mayne and fired.

Jill Mayne cried out as she saw her husband flip backwards and pieces of his left upper torso were sent spattering against the wall of the Raumschiff. Curtis Mayne hit the ground with a thud, his left shoulder gone and his left arm separated from the rest of his body. Bolt's wives instinctively ran to help the injured man. Curtis Mayne's left leg was twisted awkwardly under his body and his breathing was labored.

"What the hell!" Lancer demanded of Bolt.

"I have business on the space station!" Bolt aimed back at Jill Mayne's head. He snarled at all of the other passengers, his eyes darting back and forth between them. "Unless you want me to blow her fucking head off, you fire up those engines and get us there! Now!"

"You can't do this!" Hill protested. "The station is not safe at this time. We have to turn back! You heard what Sophia said!"

"I will kill her," Bolt promised. "Just as I killed her skinny ass husband. Turn on those engines now!"

Harriak could see in the eyes of Joseph Bolt that this was

not the first time he had killed. Harriak knew the type from his many years in the mining industry. He had seen his share of tough men and women. Bolt was a dangerous man.

Lancer looked down at Curtis Mayne who was breathing abnormally. Lancer knew the man would be dead soon. There was no doubt Bolt was a man that had no problem taking life. Bolt's wives were trying to make Mayne comfortable, one holding his hand, another stroking his hair. They were all encouraging him to hold on. Two of the Bolt wives moved Curtis Mayne's leg into a more comfortable position.

Lancer growled to the upper pilot section. "Lucius! Start up the engines again! Take us to the space station."

Lucius gave his two sisters a look of panic and silently began typing commands into the control panel before him to do as Lancer directed. They were all three speechless regarding what had happened below. Venus, who rarely wore under wear liked the way Curtis Mayne would stare at her chest when she would wear one of her skin tight half shirts without a bra. Even though the man clearly had lust in his eyes for her, they had barely said ten words to each other the whole voyage. She regretted it now, thinking it would have been fun to have an affair with Mayne. But now he was dying due to the greed of Joseph Bolt.

The engine to the Raumschiff fired back up and started moving gain, on course to Space Station Cy-5.

"Satisfied?" Lancer asked Bolt.

"Can I go get some of the medical supplies down

below?" Lila asked softly. "Maybe we can help Mister Mayne."

"Fuck him!" Bolt yelled and pointed his laser at Lila. "And you sit your ass down!"

Lila nodded and obediently sat down in one of the empty chairs. They all sat in silence as Curtis Mayne took in his last breath and his body went limp on the floor, his eyes were staring at the ceiling.

Jill Mayne sobbed over the loss of her husband. Bolt did nothing to console the grieving woman.

"You are going to get us all killed," DuBravac said flatly. "I hope that whatever it is that you hope to accomplish is worth all of our lives. When we land the soldiers will board this ship and we will be either arrested or killed on the spot."

"Maybe all of you will be," Joseph Bolt said calmly. "But not me. Now, this is how it is going to go. Lancer, Hill, Rhinehard, DuBravac and Harriak, all of you get out. When you are out of the command area I will seal it off. I will keep Jill Mayne here and the Andolini's up above as my special prisoners. You make any move to turn of the engines in the engine room or to cut of the oxygen up here then I kill the Mayne woman and the Andolini's. Got it?"

"If anything happens to my friends up there, you will be sorry." Rolf pointed up to the pilot section. "When we land I will kill you. So you better hope nothing happens. You understand me?"

"Get moving fly boy," Bolt smiled at Rolf.

Slowly the group began to leave the command section.

"Wait, not you, Lila!" Bolt yelled. "You stay here."

Lila looked at her friend DuBravac with a scared look in her eyes. She turned and walked back to where she had been sitting and waited for everyone to leave. Once the people Bolt had ordered off the command station were gone, Bolt looked to Lila.

"Seal the entrance."

Lila did as instructed and pressed a red button on the wall which caused a thick metal bulkhead to slide down and deal off the command station from the lower levels of the ship.

"Sit," Bolt instructed her.

She sat down as he had demanded.

Bolt looked at his eight wives and smiled at them. "I am doing this for all of us. We will be rich after I finish the deal on Cy-5."

Minxia Lu Bolt looked down at the corpse of Curtis Mayne and shook her head sadly. "By killing this man you bring dishonor to our family. You did not have to do that."

"Honor? You can't eat honor. Honor does not buy all that nice jewelry I provide to you and your sister wives. Honor does not put a roof over your head. You bitches need to learn that." Bolt pushed the weeping Mayne widow into the chair next to him. "If you move, you die. Understand me?"

Jill Mayne nodded that she understood.

Minxia and six of the other wives of Bolt began removing their necklaces, bracelets, earrings, rings and other assorted jewelry and placing the items on the command desk in front of Bolt. The only wife that did not remove her expensive diamonds and gems was Anna Bolt. She watched her sister wives in disbelief as they all voluntarily removed the priceless jewelry.

"We will not wear these items if it means people must be harmed for us to have them," Minxia announced defiantly.

Anna Bolt walked over to Joseph Bolt and stood next to him. She glared at her sister wives. Before being sold to Bolt, Anna had been raised in an orphanage. She had no possessions throughout her life until Bolt showered her with jewelry. Never in her life had she had so many possessions. She could not understand the reaction of Minxia and the others. "I am with you my husband."

Joseph Bolt sneered at the seven wives that were throwing his generosity back at him. "Stupid women. Fine, when we get to the Space Station I will divorce you all, except for Anna here. I will have no problem finding replacement wives for you."

Anna Bolt smiled at him, "There are two up the ladder that would make fine wives."

"Yes. Yes they would. Andolini girls!" Bolt yelled at the pilot section. "Get your sexy booties down here or Lila gets her head blown off."

Giola and Venus exchanged looks of concern. They knew without words being exchanged that they could not leave Lila alone with that lunatic. Both girls quietly climbed down the ladder from the pilot section to the large command section. They saw the body of Curtis Mayne on the floor his left arm lying a few feet away.

Bolt looked the two Italian women over, smiling at their shapely legs and full breasts. "Yes, I think they would make great wives. Both of you, strip."

"Excuse me?" Giola raised her eyebrows. In her modeling career she was accustomed to photographers or men with money asking her to undress. But they would normally ask nicely or promise more money for the photo shoot if she and her two sisters went nude. Bolt was not asking. He was demanding with a threat of violence if they failed to comply.

"Take off your clothes. I want to inspect the merchandise before I make an offer to your family to purchase you." Bolt ordered. "I will count to ten and both of you had better be naked or Lila there loses her head."

"My father and brothers would rip your cock off if you spoke to them about us in such a manner." Venus hissed at him. She had a strong desire to leap at him and scratch out his eyes.

The Andolini girls looked at each other as if stunned as Bolt sighed and aimed his laser pistol at Lila's head. "One. Two. Three."

"Okay!" Venus said and walked over to stand in front of Lila. "Just leave everyone alone."

"Do it," Bolt ordered.

The two Andolini girls pulled off their red sweaters revealing their full breasts and flat stomachs. Bolt licked his lips. "Oh yes. You both would be fantastic wives. I will pay your father top dollar."

"You clearly do not know our father," Venus told him.

"You are an evil man," Lila hissed.

"Excuse me?" Bolt smiled and aimed the laser pistol at her direction.

"I said you are evil. My mother told me about men like you. She said that you are all shameful and lacking in morals. The Gods will punish you for killing Mr. Mayne."

Bolt laughed, "Morals? When you are dead that is all that there is, you stupid girl. There are no Gods and there is no afterlife. So, I enjoy myself while I am breathing. If I want to shoot someone then I will do it. If I want to take a woman for my pleasure then I will do so. Whether the woman submits willingly or not is her problem. I do as I wish."

"What gives you the right to take life?" Minxia challenged him.

Bolt grinned, "This laser pistol in my hands gives me the right to do whatever I wish."

In the lower level of the Raumschiff, DuBravac and Rolf found Jurgen, Harcourt, Porter and Choi calmly playing cards in the lower level break room.

"On your feet boys," DuBravac barked as she walked into the room. "We have ourselves a little situation."

"What is going on?" Porter sat his two cards down on the table.

"Joseph Bolt is a psycho," Rolf told them. "He took hostages in the command level and killed a passenger."

"Where is Lila?" Jurgen stood up. "Is she up there?" He began to run to the entrance only to have Rolf stop him by grabbing his shoulders.

"Calm down, mein freund." Rolf said softly. "Yes she is up there. But she is okay right now. All three of the Andolini's are there, too."

"What can we do?" Choi demanded.

"Nothing," DuBravac said, pacing back and forth like a caged tiger. "We have to hope he doesn't kill anyone else. Damn. And if we keep flying on our current heading we will be in range of the space station soon. We won't be able to turn back without raising suspicions."

"Suspicions about what?" Harcourt was on his feet, his eyes closed and his brow furrowed as he was concentrating.

"About us," DuBravac kept her pacing. "The Station is in the middle of a civil war. They are arresting everyone. Les said they are killing Christians like nothing. He warned us to go home and Bolt just went crazy. He took a hostage and killed Mister Mayne. He ordered the rest of us out and then sealed the bulkheads!"

"Shhhh." Harcourt told them, his eyes still shut.

"What the hell are you doing, Jack?" Rolf demanded.

"I am trying to read Joseph Bolt's mind. May I have some silence please? I cannot concentrate if the rest of you are babbling," Harcourt requested.

Harcourt hated to use his powers as a Child of Athena. He felt the abilities were a curse. But in a time when his friends were in danger, he was not going to stand by and do nothing. He found the mind of Minxia Bolt and saw through her eyes. Joseph Bolt was forcing the Andolini girls to undress. They were both naked. Bolt was demanding that they give him a lap dance. Harcourt slowly moved his concentration around the room upstairs and entered the mind of Joseph Bolt.

Choi, Porter, Rolf and DuBravac watched in silence as Harcourt leaned up against the wall. He was shaking and his legs were beginning to bend underneath him. One of the draw backs of reading another person's mind was that the effort drained the physical strength of the Harcourt. He felt the muscular body of Rolf steady him and lead him to a chair. Harcourt sat down and his mind touched the mind of Joseph Bolt. He heard Bolt demand that Giola perform oral sex on him. She was refusing. Bolt aimed his laser at Lila and threatened to kill her if Giola did not do as he asked. Harcourt clenched his fists and began the process of trying to control Bolt's thoughts and will.

The Andolini twin girls had removed all of their clothes and were refusing to perform sex acts on Bolt. He aimed his laser at Lila and threatened her life.

"Okay," Venus said softly. "You win. I'll do it."

"No," Bolt smiled. "I want your sister to do it. I can tell you have more experience with men than her. So, I want your sister to do it."

"But due to my experience I can better pleasure you," Venus protested. "I once did three guys in one night. My sister doesn't have my level of experience."

"No," Bolt said and he seemingly froze in front of them all. He felt himself lose all control of his thought process. His muscles would not respond and he felt as if he had been turned into stone. Bolt wanted to pull the trigger of his laser pistol, but something prohibited him from doing so.

The other watched his eyes grow glassy, staring off at nothing in particular. Bolt slowly lowered his laser pistol to the table and to their shock he slid the pistol toward Lila. She immediately grabbed hold of the weapon and aimed it at Bolt.

Rolf regarded Harcourt's face and could see the strain on it. Harcourt was perspiring a white colored sweat, grinding his teeth and shaking as if he were freezing. Using his mental control powers, Harcourt forced Bolt to lower the hand laser to the table.

Giola and Venus began to dress quickly.

"What is wrong with him?" Venus wondered out loud. "He looks like he is in some sort of a trance."

"Like he was hypnotized," Lila observed as she kept the laser aimed at him. She was determined to pull the trigger if the evil man moved.

Anna Bolt shook her husband. "Joseph! What is wrong with you! Joseph!"

Minxia ran to the bulkhead controls and pressed the button. She was relieved to see that Harriak, Lancer and Hill were there waiting. The three men charged in and began punching Bolt senseless. Anna Bolt scratched Hill in the face with her long fingernails in an effort to defend her husband. Jill Mayne punched Anna Bolt in the nose. The blow had enough force to send Anna Bolt falling backwards onto the metal floor.

Lancer used plastic ties to bind Joseph Bolt's wrists and ankles. "James, get up there and help Lucius turn this ship around. If the space station picked us up on their long range scans, we could be toast."

Hill ascended the ladder and sat down in the co-pilot seat next to Lucius.

"My sisters..." Lucius said softly. "Are they okay?"

Hill slapped him on the shoulder. "They are fine, kid. You did well."

Lucius felt like he had let his sisters down by not doing something to protect them. Bolt was going to violate them and he sat in his pilot's seat frozen like a block of ice.

Hill was punching buttons on the command board as fast as he could. He looked up from the panel and swallowed hard. "Ah, shit."

"What happened?" Lucius asked.

"They got a lock on us and have dispatched three small fighter ships to bring us in or blow us to hell. Gillis was right. We are screwed." Hill stood up and leaned his head down the ladder shaft and yelled to Lancer, "They are on to us. They sent interception ships. If we try and run, they will blow us up."

Lancer kicked Joseph Bolt in the ribs. "Asshole. Now we are in big trouble."

"Can't we fight them?" Lila asked naively.

"Yes we could and we would win. But then they would send ten more ships and then we would be dead." Lancer sighed as he verbally played out the scenario. "Let's cooperate with them fully. Maybe we can find a way out of this."

Jurgen ran up the stairs and found his wife. He took her in his arms and held her tight. They kissed over and over again. "Thank the Stars you are safe."

Down below, Harcourt had exhausted himself with his mind control trick on Bolt. Harcourt set his head down and was asleep in seconds. Rolf lifted Harcourt up in his arms and carried him to his sleeping quarters. None of the other cadets had ever seen a Harcourt use their special powers before. Each had a new found respect for their friend Jack Harcourt.

Lancer and Harriak carried Joseph and Anna Bolt to a special room located on the lower level of the Raumschiff and locked the two inside. It was a living quarter that Lancer had converted into a mini-prison for situations in which a passenger got out of line. The door locking mechanism was one that he had personally installed and it would only open or close based on Lancer's voice command. After locking the metal doors, Lancer rushed back up to the command area and then climbed the ladder to the pilot section. He overheard hear his longtime friend, James Hill, trying to negotiate with the commander of Station Cy-5.

"Let me handle it, Jimmy." Lancer intervened.

"Good luck," Hill shrugged. "He is an asshole."

Lancer took the wireless microphone from the command console and switched the conversation so that it would be heard throughout the Raumschiff. He felt he owed it to the passengers to know exactly what they were facing.

"This is Captain Lancer. Who am I speaking with?"

"I am Captain Antonin Sikorsky of the UNSC and commanding officer of the Space Station Cy-5. You are ordered to accompany the escort of ships that I have dispatched to your location. They will lead you to the main Docking Bay of the Space Station. Do you copy?"

"I copy," Lancer responded. "We will comply with your orders."

"Good. Because if you deviate from the course, my fighters have standing orders to open fire on your ship with R-5 armor piercing rockets. Sikorsky out."

Lancer made certain the communications were severed before he addressed Hill and Lucius. His leaned his forehead close to them both and whispered so that any eavesdroppers below the pilot section would not hear. His hope was to avoid panic among the passengers by addressing them face to face and attempt to reassure them that all was not lost. "You two stay here and keep the ship going. Do whatever they order you to do. I am going down below. I think it is time to arm everyone."

Lancer slid down the ladder and saw the seven remaining Bolt wives with Rolf and the Andolini sisters waiting for him. Many of them had fear in their eyes. Some had a silent determination about them. Venus looked plain angry.

"We heard the Captain on the space station," Rolf told Lancer. "If we dock, they will kill several of us, if not all."

"They can die trying," Lancer responded. "I know you cadets get weapons training at the Academy. How about you ladies?"

Minxia shook her head, "No, we were all house wives. We never even saw a laser pistol before today."

Lancer pursed his lips and nodded. They had a little bit of time before they docked on the space station. Those that knew how to fire a weapon would have to take the time to teach the others what to do. "All right then, class is in session. All of you follow me to the lower level."

"What is down there?" Venus wanted to know.

"Weapons and lots of them," Lancer told them. "When we dock, we come out and start blasting. If we die today then we make sure we do some damage in return."

Giola blinked at that statement. She was far past wishing she had not left New Edinburgh to join the trip. "So they are going to kill us?"

"Most likely," Rolf said as he followed Lancer.

The women followed the two men down the winding stair case to the lower level. Lancer stopped at the back exit ramp on the Raumschiff loading area. He pulled out a key ring from his breast pocket and began unlocking several floor mechanisms to release the fasteners to his secret storage area. Lancer then pushed the metal floor to the south of the ship to reveal a compartment with footlockers full of hand lasers, laser rifles and many other types of weapons.

"Wow," Giola said softly.

"Tell Sophia and the others to get down here and arm themselves," Lancer ordered. "Rolf, you and Sophia teach these Bolt women how to use the hand lasers. We don't have time to teach them anything else."

"So our husband is dead?" Mixia asked.

"Not yet," Lancer winked at her. "But he will be very soon."

Giola took a hand laser and laser rifle and walked away from the others without saying a word. She walked up the ramp that led to the sleeping quarters and found the room she had been sharing with her sister, Venus. She set her two weapons on the floor and sat down on her bed. She covered her face with her hands and began crying. She was not ready to die. She had so many things that she had wanted to do in her life. She had wanted to graduate from the Academy like her two older brothers had done. She wanted to see her parents look at her with pride in their eyes.

"Are you okay?" Norman Porter asked Giola. He had been walking past her room when he heard her crying. She had been his friend since he joined the Academy and moved to planet New Edinburgh. The lovely Italian woman had invited him to family cook outs and other gatherings. Porter felt indebted to the beautiful woman and hated to see her so distraught.

Giola shook her head from left to right and looked up at the kind face of Porter. "They are going to kill us on that space station. I'm not ready to die."

Porter walked over and sat down on the bed next to her.

He put his right arm over her shoulders to console her. "None of us are. Don't give up hope, Giola. Miracles do happen."

"Miracles? We are in the middle of outer space, being forced to land on a hostile space station so that we can be executed. It is hopeless."

Porter wiped the tears from her face, "Yes I believe in miracles. Your brother Marco was thought dead on the Blood Moon but he survived. Les Gillis is on that space station and although I never met him, I bet when he finds out his wife is in trouble he will be there."

Giola tried to smile at that. "That's good for Sophia. She has a hero to fight for her. I never had a man love me like that. When I was younger I remember seeing Les and Sophia together. The way they looked at each other. There was always love between them. I guess I will never know what it is like to have a man love me that way."

Porter looked down for a second and then raised his eyes again. "Giola, you are only eighteen. You will find a love like that. Every single guy at the Academy loves you and your sisters. You and Venus are the most beautiful women I have ever known. You could make any man of your choice love you."

Giola thought about Porter's words for a moment. "And you, Norman? Could you love Venus? Or me?"

"I already do love you both," he admitted softly. "Your family has been wonderful to me. I would do anything for you two."

Giola whispered in his ear, "Well then, Norman, I would

like you to make love to me. If we are going to die, then I don't want to die a virgin. Close the door, Computer."

Porter swallowed and was about to say yes when Giola began kissing him. Porter wrapped his arms around her and was kissing her passionately. The sliding doors to the room entrance slammed shut. Giola stood up in front of Porter and pulled off her sweater revealing her body to him. Porter pulled her back onto the bed, kissing her all over. They made love together as the rest of the members of Lancer's ship were practicing how to defend themselves.

CHAPTER SIX

Gillis was grateful for the way that the Ortiz family and the Bauslaugh pack of human-feline hybrids had saved his life. He was even more indebted to them for the manner in which they assisted him in warning his wife to avoid Space Station Cy-5 at any cost. But even with all that Gillis felt he owed these people, they were demanding something that he felt was far too risky. All of the thirteen Ortiz family members wanted to take control of the space station. The Bauslaugh clan had agreed with their plan. Gillis advised against such course of action.

The debate got heated quickly. The bar that was owned by the Ortiz family was full of likeminded individuals that wanted to kill the soldiers of the Glorious Leader and obtain freedom. Gillis was in the center of the bar named Dos Gueros Muertos. To his left were about thirty round and rectangular shaped tables full of members of the Kotek Bauslaugh family. To his right were the thirteen Ortiz family members and a crowd of other humans that had joined their cause. Some were there due to family members having been killed or arrested. Others were wanted criminals for treason or other acts and they thought that overthrowing the government might absolve them of their sins. Others were there out of family loyalty. Some were there just because they enjoyed a good fight.

Gillis was there because the MI had attempted to arrest him the moment he arrived on the space station. The Kotek's to his left had rescued him from certain torture in the Tank, which was the name of the space station prison. Gillis motioned for the crowd to calm down. They were all screaming at Gillis accusing him of being a coward or a loyalist to the Sikorsky family. All of the anger directed at him was due to his conclusion that their best course of action was to flee the station as opposed to attempt to take control of it.

Gillis looked over to the Kotek's. He had to remember not to refer to them as Kotek for they hated the name. They preferred terms like enhanced humans or simply to be referred to by their birth names. Their family leader was called Dracula. He was the father and grandfather of the large number of furry human-feline looking creatures. They were all double jointed in their wrists, elbows, ankles and knees which enabled them to walk upright or drop down on all fours and run just as a lion or leopard would. Their ears were similar to that of a cat as were their eyes. They had whiskers and their teeth were sharp. On their hands and feet, or paws as some referred to them, they had sharp claws that were quite deadly in battle. Each of them had long tails that they used as a tool for holding onto pipes or ladders or other objects that they could swing on. Their tails were also strong enough to wrap around a man and lift him into the air. The Bauslaugh family was mostly hybrids but some of the pack had bred with human men and females which caused their offspring to have more human features.

Gillis had met them all. Dracula was solid black with yellow eyes and taller than most of the others. His wife, Panther, was also solid black, slender and fast. Gillis realized quickly that she liked to talk often. They had many of their children present with them. There was the first litter of Dracula and Panther that consisted of CJ, Tuxedo, Summer, Angel, Velvet and Luna. CJ had two litters; the first group consisted of Midnight, Ebony, Merlin and Arthur. Her second litter consisted of Snowflake, Wolvie, Odysseus, Mittens and Phoenix. The only reason Gillis could remember their names was because of the story behind them or the names were descriptive of their color or look. Wolvie, for example, had solid black hair, light eyes, with thick fur that made him look like a wolf. His tail was thick and Wolvie was constantly having to brush it with a special comb. Snowflake was solid white with light blue eyes and seemed to have the all of human women in love with him. He was always sitting in some pretty ladies lap, purring as they scratched him under his chin or behind his ears. Mittens was black with white paws and a spot of white on his face and under his chin. Midnight and Ebony were solid black with yellow eyes. Merlin and Arthur had patches of black and white that made no geometric sense.

The only other Kotek that Gillis could recall the name to be was the one named Napoleon or Nappy for short. He was large, calico colored, with dark lines around his eyes that made him look like a raccoon and he had a thick, bushy tail. Nappy seemed to be a brilliant engineer from the way he would discuss building ships or repairing them.

Mittens seemed to favor Gillis as he was constantly bringing him a pink and white fluffy ball for him to throw. Gillis would toss the ball and Mittens would charge after it and grab it in his mouth looking at his siblings and cousins as if challenging them to try and take it from him.

In the short time that Gillis had been associating with the cat family he had learned that not only were they acrobatic and lethal fighters, but they were each well-read and intelligent. Most of them were engineers. Luna, Velvet, Panther and CJ were doctors. Odysseus was studying on line computer classes to learn geological explorations. Dracula and others were acrobats as well and toured the eight solar systems putting on live performances for paying audiences. Business was good and the family had a good flow of income. The one named BB that Gillis had met on the transport ship was present as well. He smiled at Gillis and waived his hand of dark fur at him.

Gillis nodded back at him as he was happy to see the friendly young Kotek again. In their short conversation that they had on their first meeting, Gillis had found BB to be amiable and smart. He hoped to get to know him better.

Each of the Bauslaugh family members wore black sleeveless tops and white shorts that had a small hole in the back so that their tails were able to be free of encumbrances. They were interesting to watch as they all exhibited human personality traits as well as feline attributes. Gillis had seen them purr and enjoy being scratched under their chins or behind their ears. They also would lick each other in order to clean one another or show affection.

On the other side of the room were the screaming humans led by the Ortiz family. The father of the twelve siblings was Joseph Ortiz, also known as Joe. He was in his early fifties, a bit overweight, had a receding hairline, dark eyes and walked with a slight limp. He was wearing a white dress shirt that was not tucked into his black trousers. He held a place of respect among all of the freedom fighters that were in the bar. His brother had been a rebel that died on the moon named Chronos when the Glorious Leader ordered one of the Red Javelin Weapons to be detonated there.

Ortiz had one son, named Junior, who was in his early twenties, handsome, tall slender in build with thick dark hair and eyes. His sisters would tease him that he had inherited their mothers' hair. He was adept at weapons but had mainly learned the bar business so that he could help the expanding Ortiz family empire of opening new Dos Gueros Muertos locations throughout the eight solar systems. Junior had never married but he was involved with a few of the other females that were screaming for liberty. He was wearing a dark purple turtle neck sweater with black slacks and black leather boots.

The eleven sisters were all attractive. Gillis had met

and spoke with Amy and Karla Ortiz at length. Both of them seemed to understand his fears for initiating a full scale war on the space station. But they were afraid to openly support his unpopular advice on the subject. Both had offered to marry Gillis so that they could make babies for the hero of the Blood Moon. Even though Gillis had explained that he had a wife already the two women continued to pursue him. Each of the ladies had dark hair and brown eyes, slim and stood just a few inches over five feet tall.

Karla Ortiz had her dark hair up in a hair clip. She had on a matching set of oval garnet earrings and necklace. Her dark slacks hugged her figure in a complimentary fashion and her white button down blouse was loose fitting and tucked under her pants. She had a nice smile and full lips. She had an Ak-47 machine gun slung over her right shoulder and a green back pack over her right. The back pack was full of extra ammo clips, a laser pistol, some grenades and other weapons.

Amy Ortiz wore her hair loose and had silver tear drop earrings on. She had on a dark brown sweater with khaki pants and black boots. She had a thick military belt around her waist that had a large hunting knife, a laser pistol and two pouches filled with flame darts and stun darts. She had laid a laser pistol down on the table top before her and her arms were crossed as she watched the scene with interest.

Gillis thought had he never met Sophia he might have been receptive to the advances of the two Ortiz women. But he knew Sophia would kill both girls in a bad way before she turned on him.

The other sisters were from two large birthing groups. There were five sisters that were twenty years old named Estrella, Sara, Krista, Nina and Melody. There were four other sisters that were seventeen years old named Tina, Erika, Catrina and Mandy. All of the Ortiz sisters had dark hair save Sara who had her hair dyed blonde. Melody had some dark red highlights in her long hair. They were each about the same height and build except Amy who was more curvaceous than all of her sisters.

Each of the Ortiz girls knew the restaurant and bar business well. But they were not soldiers and had little to no training in combat or self-defense. Amy and Karla knew some martial arts and both knew how to fire weapons. Junior Ortiz had also learned how to fight with laser pistols by paying for lessons at a target range. Krista and Nina had also attended some martial arts courses but they were not even close to a black belt. Krista had her green belt and was quite proud of that fact. Nina was still in her white belt.

The other humans were a rag tag group of criminals and downtrodden. Gillis knew that the only chance they had was to board and steal one of the ships in the docking area or make a bold move to invade the Science Cruiser *Wisconsin* that had been docked next to the space station. The screams of coward and traitor had subsided as Gillis kept asking the crowd to listen to him. He had to get through to them all, otherwise they were likely to take an offensive action that would get them all killed.

"I don't understand you!" Junior Ortiz pointed his finger in Gillis' direction. "If we take the Command Station then we control the space station. We should be able to do that easily!"

"No!" Gillis shouted back at him and leaned forward on the table before him. "The power in any space station or battle cruiser is in the engine room and life support section. If we do anything, that should be your focus. But the better plan is to get everyone out of here in a couple of Raumschiffs. If we storm the docking area, locate two to three of those style of ships, we can board and fly off before the weapons section can fire on us. That is our only option."

One of the females stood up screaming. She was dressed in a blood stained black Military Intelligence uniform that had been taken from a dead combatant. "My husband and children are in the Tank! You are saying that I should just abandon them? Hell no!"

"My wife and kids are also in the Tank!" A man with the tattoo of the cross on his face shouted. He was wearing a simple green t-shirt with light brown shorts and slippers on his feet.

"Please, everyone, please!" Blu raised her voice. She was dressed in one of the MI uniforms and had cut a slit in the back so her tail could have freedom of movement. She had a beautiful coat of dark blue fur and was three quarters human and one forth feline. Her features were quite attractive and she exuded confidence as she addressed the crowd. "We need to listen to Mr. Gillis. He has fought in a life and death situation before. Few of us have his experience or education. So I suggest we heed his advice."

"We must find a way off this death trap," Gillis told them all as he smiled at Blu to acknowledge her. "Fighting to control this station is one thing. But we would all be sitting ducks out here in deep space. Think about it. The Glorious Leader just wiped out over eight hundred thousand people on a moon. Do any of you think for a second that he would not hesitate to blast this station to pieces? Do you? We need to procure ships that are mobile and give ourselves a chance to outrun our enemy. This station is stuck in constant orbit. For the enemy it would be like shouting apples in a barrel. We would all be dead in no time."

"And the current engineering warnings indicate that there are several hull breaches on the space station," Midnight informed the group. "If this station takes any more direct hits, the hull could begin to split apart. That would cause explosive decompression, rapid decrease in the breathable oxygen levels which would cause all of us to be torn out into space and we would be dead in seconds. I agree with Les. We need to get off of this station and find a more defensible location."

Karla Ortiz cleared her throat and approached the front and stood next to Gillis. She had her holographic-communication device in her right hand and there was a three dimensional news report emanating from hit. "I am afraid he is right. I am looking at my holo-com and the current news reports. Everyone here should watch what has just happened. The Glorious Leader fired nuclear missiles on the entire Second Fleet. He has also ordered that more population centers be wiped out by those Red Javelin things. He is going to commit eleven more acts of planetacide."

Gillis grimaced at her news report and pulled out his own hand held computer to see for himself. The rest of the occupants of the bar did the same. Gillis watched the replay as the *Amistad* was shot at from its' rear by a ship that the news media termed as a "Stealth Battle Cruiser." He closed his eyes as the doomed Battle Cruiser was vaporized with all life on board when the nuclear weapons detonated. He remained silent as each of the other Second Fleet Battle Cruisers was destroyed in a similar manner. Many in the crowd listened to the last words of Dana Del Rey as she begged for mercy just before her ship was similarly fired upon. Gillis looked down at the floor and thought of his friends in the Second Fleet: Dia Cho, Felicia Essex, Ellen Benson and Marco Andolini. Gillis grimaced with rage as he thought of their faces. He recalled their laughs, the sounds of their voices their past conversations and their hopes for the future. He remembered how Cho and Essex had been so radiant and beautiful on their wedding day. They had been so happy together.

Gillis also recalled how Marco and Benson had fought so bravely on the Blood Moon. They had been his friends. Gillis did not realize that the crowd was silent, all eyes were on him with a looks of hope and despair. Gillis felt warm tears running down his cheeks as he mourned for his four lost friends. He looked up at the crowd and observed that many of them were also moved to tears. It had been a massacre. Gillis nodded and was about to speak when he felt his personal communication device vibrating.

"Answer," Gillis instructed his small computer.

"Les, mi amour!" It was his wife, Sophia. Her voice sounded desperate.

"Sophia! Are you and the Blues City on the way back to New Edinburgh?"

"No," she informed him. "We are being forced to land on the space station! We are surrounded by four Allen Type Fighters. Giles Lancer felt it best not to try and take them on and land as ordered. I am so sorry."

"No honey, I am sorry. We should have known that the political climate was boiling to this point." Gillis sat down in a chair as he felt himself overwhelmed by the loss of four friends and now his wife was in imminent danger. "We all should have stayed home and waited to see what would happen. How long until you arrive?"

"James Hill said we will be there in about fifteen minutes," she responded.

Gillis was silent for a few moments. The gathering at Dos Gueros Muertos was listening intently to the conversation. Many of the group was still speechless at the demise of the crews of the Second Fleet. Their hopes that the blockade would be successful had been dashed by the destruction of Admiral Khan's ships. Others were left without words as the world's being targeted for extinction by the Glorious Leader were their home planets. Plus the word that the moon called Robert Andrews was going to be annihilated resonated throughout the entire bar. That moon was close in proximity to Space Station Cy-5 and no one knew whether the Red Javelin weapon would cause enough destructive energy to reach them as well.

"Honey?" DuBravac asked out loud. "Are you still there?"

"Yes," he finally spoke as he had been lost in his thoughts, trying to formulate a plan of action to save his wife and friends. "Sophia, tell Lancer to do nothing. If I know him he is planning some form of futile heroics that will get you all killed. Land, cooperate with the MI soldiers that will meet you at the docking area and wait for me to find you. I will find all of you."

"But they might kill us all," she said softly.

"Over my dead body," Gillis swore. His thoughts

were going over several scenarios in which he could lead a few Bauslaugh family members on a rescue attempt. The only chance that Gillis had to save his wife and friends was if they landed safely on the space station. He could do nothing as long as they were out in space. "Tell Lancer I said to do nothing but to cooperate. That is the best chance for everyone to walk away. Tell him."

"I will."

"I love you, Sophia."

"I love you too, Les. I will be waiting for you."

Her image faded away and Gillis sat in silence.

"What do we do now? Rowr!" CJ rubbed her furry face on Gillis' shoulder.

He waited for a moment to compose himself. He had not expected that his wife and friends would be forced to land on the space station. Gillis knew that Jurgen and his wife, Lila, were passengers on the *Blues City*. He did not know all of the passengers, but the fact that three Andolini's were also coming made him feel stressed even more. The Andolini family had been good ambassadors of the foreign students at Clovis Academy. The Andolini girls affectionately called Gillis "Uncle Les" as they considered him not just a friend, but as family. They had made his freshman year at the Academy a pleasant experience due to their kindness and hospitality.

Gillis slowly stood up, "Okay. You all want to take the station? I suppose current events have forced my hand. But my reasons are now selfish in nature. I have to protect my wife and friends. I think we should split up into three groups."

"And do what?" Midnight growled.

"One group to take the engineering station which houses the life support machines. So, we need all of you with any experience in engineering or oxygen regeneration machinery to go with that group." Gillis looked over each of the members as he spoke.

"Meeoow. The second group?" Luna asked.

"The second group will have to fight to secure the weapons section. That will be the most dangerous mission. It will be fully operational with Technical operatives, tactical specialists, Marines and MI soldiers on guard. I suspect that there will be a high probability for numerous casualties on that mission." Gillis warned them.

"And the third mission?" Summer asked, blinking her blue cats eyes at Gillis.

"The third mission I am going on alone. I am going to disrupt the docking bay to give my wife and friends a fighting chance to survive." Gillis picked up a hand laser on the table before him and gripped it in his right hand. He grabbed the ancient looking Japanese sword that he had picked out earlier when Karla Ortiz showed off their arsenal to him. "My wife is a good engineer and so are a few of her friends. Take the engine room and wait for us. When we arrive Sophia, Lila and Jurgen can gas the rest of the station into submission. Any questions?"

Midnight looked at his father. Dracula hissed, "You are not going alone, Les Gillis. Take Midnight, Mittens, BB and Nappy with you. They are some of our best fighters and you will need them."

"I am going with you, too." Karla Ortiz announced. "That gives you an army of six."

"And with the element of surprise on our side, perhaps that will be enough." Gillis smiled. He nodded at Dracula and Midnight. "Thank you."

"Lead on," Midnight growled as he stood up on his hind legs.

"Before we go, consider this." Gillis addressed the gathering. "If we take this station, we free all of the prisoners in the Tank. Docked to this station is a science vessel that is as big as a battle cruiser and it has limited offensive capability. Think about joining me in taking that ship and leaving this place. In this kind of warfare it is better to be mobile. Think about it."

"You seem to be, what is the word I am looking for, prescient?" Blu asked Gillis. "Have you faced such a situation in your past?"

"No, not like this," Gillis responded to her. "But I have read about space stations that take too many hits from missile fire. Their hulls can split, almost like taking a piece of paper and tearing it. I am not prescient as you suggest, but I have studied past wars and battles. We do not want to be on this station if the outer hull begins to crack open. As Midnight pointed out, we would all be dead very quickly."

Joe Ortiz hugged Gillis and then his daughter Karla as they began to leave. Dracula and Panther began meowing in loud voices to their family members, splitting them up among those that knew how to work on engines and those that were good fighters. The Ortiz family and the remaining humans began to do the same. It was time to fight.

Gillis led Midnight, BB, Mittens, Nappy and Karla Ortiz out the front door to Dos Gueros Muertos and into the long transparent metal hallway that went east and west from the bar. The hallway was about twenty feet wide and the ceiling above was approximately forty feet high as most of the businesses located on that level of the space station had two floors of space. To the north was the protective transparent metal rails that were about four feet tall. Past that was a drop of two hundred feet to the lower level of the station.

Gillis made it just two steps outside when he heard the words that made his heart skip a beat.

"Freeze! Drop all of your weapons!" The words echoed all around them.

Gillis stopped in his tracks and looked east and west. On either side of him there were about forty Marines. Some of them were prone, others on one knee and the rest standing. They were all aiming laser rifles in their direction. Gillis cursed at himself for not having the foresight to ask Ortiz if there were any other exits from Dos Gueros Muertos. Even the dim witted MI was capable of figuring out where the saboteurs had been hiding out. Gillis dropped his sword and pistol to the floor and raised his hand.

Behind him, he could hear Midnight growling. His fangs were barred, his ears were bent at an angle and his fur on his back was up. He was starting to go into a crouch, presumably to begin a charge at the Marines on either the west or east side of them.

"Calm down there. This is not the time to give up

your life," Gillis whispered to the solid black furred Kotek.

Midnight glared at Gillis with his yellow cat's eyes, "They are going to kill us anyway. I would rather go out ripping open their throats."

"Stand down, my friend. We'll get our chance," Gillis said calmly as he surveyed the soldiers that had surrounded them. "Our day will come."

Midnight reluctantly raised his muscular arms into the sky. BB, Mittens and Nappy followed suit. Karla slowly knelt down to the metal walkway and laid down her Uzi machine gun and three knives that were in sheaths around her belt. She looked scared, especially in her eyes. They had walked right into an ambush. All the Marine commander had to say was the word and all six would be dead in seconds. She looked over her shoulder and saw that her father was standing in the doorway of Dos Gueros Muertos, looking to her for direction. Karla shook her head side to side to warn him not to come out into the hallway.

"State your name!" The same voice boomed from the east side of the hallway.

Gillis cleared his throat. He was most likely going to be arrested for the death of Jenssen when Dracula and some of his family ripped the man to shreds. With the state of the art cameras and photography on the space station, there was nothing to be gained by attempting to conceal his identity. "Les Gillis."

"Les Gillis?" the voice rang out. "The Les Gillis from Clovis Academy?"

"Yes," Gillis answered back. He detected a French accent in the mystery voice.

"Stand down," the voice ordered. "Marines, shoulder your weapons! Stand down!"

Gillis and Karla exchanged confused looks. Midnight meowed to BB, Mittens and Nappy telling them to slowly start moving sideways in case they needed to attack.

The hallway was silent as a Marine from the back of the soldiers stepped forward. Gillis looked at the man that was walking toward him. He was over six feet tall, muscular and his hands had no weapon. He was wearing the camouflaged fatigues that were the standard dress for the Space Command Marines. Gillis saw First Lieutenant rank insignias on his collar and the patch on his shoulders indicated that he was a member of the crew of the Science Cruiser *Wisconsin*. He had on a black beret that covered the top of his head. Gillis was forced to do a double take when he focused his gaze on the man's face.

"Shit," Gillis whispered to the other four with him

on the hallway.

"What is it?" Karla whispered back.

"He used to be in a gang that I fought against back in the Academy," Gillis answered her. "This might not go over well for us."

Gillis watched as First Lieutenant Francois Zerbe walked closer to them. "I am unarmed. I just want to talk."

Gillis remembered Zerbe well from all of the rumbles they had against each other years back. Zerbe had been a cadet senior while Gillis had been a freshman. Zerbe was one of the founders of what came to be known as the Bragg Gang. There had been no love lost between Gillis and Francois Zerbe during the one year they knew each other. Zerbe had been abusive of other underclassmen and the Gorski Gang stood against him on many occasions. Zerbe had left Clovis Academy before Gillis began his second year. Gillis had lost touch with the man after he graduated from the Academy. In his last year at the Academy, Gillis did befriend Zerbe's younger brother, Pierre. Pierre had gone to the Blood Moon as part of the team to compete against three other schools. None of them had realized that an ambush was waiting for them. Pierre had been the first of the Clovis Academy cadets to die. Gillis recalled the death of Pierre like it was just yesterday.

He vividly recalled his last seconds as he was gasping for air as his blood filled his lungs.

Francois Zerbe was handsome and had many lovers. He was a professional womanizer and had left a trail of broken hearts from Clovis City to every port that his science cruiser visited. He had slept with just about every one of the Bragg Gang girls. He had even been active with several of the women that served on the same ship he had. In addition to his sexual conquests, Zerbe was a formidable hand to hand opponent. Gillis remembered the many fights between the Gorski Gang and the Bragg Gang. They always ended in arrests, broken furniture and an occasional injury or two. Gillis was certain that Zerbe would be wanting to settle the score with him. Gillis balled up his fists, just in case.

Zerbe stopped in front of the six would be rebels. He looked over BB, Midnight, Nappy and Mittens. He had never been so close to a Kotek before. He was taken in how their cat faces possessed many human characteristics. He had heard from other soldiers and pilots that sex with a Kotek was an amazing experience. Zerbe took the four before him as males so any ideas of sexual advances with them was out. "Cute."

He then let his eyes wander over to Karla Ortiz. She fidgeted as she realized he was undressing her with his eyes. Zerbe liked her face, her figure and the way she looked him in the eyes without diverting her gaze. She had self-confidence and a little fire in her eyes.

"Very nice," Zerbe commented to her.

Gillis glared at Zerbe and pointed his index finger at him. "You said you wanted to talk?"

Zerbe looked down at Gillis and nodded, "Were you there?"

"There for what?"

"When my brother died?"

Gillis nodded slowly as he recalled the tragic ambush of the slave Saharakaree aliens on the Blood Moon. Eamon O'Grady was injured in that battle and Pierre Zerbe had died. "Yes, I was there to hear his last words. He was my friend. Of course I was there. I wasn't going to let him die alone."

Zerbe looked up at the ceiling and nodded. He had never appreciated his younger brother as he should have when he was alive. He always belittled him and took him for granted. Now that Pierre was gone, Francois felt as if he was not whole. The death of his brother made him feel as if he was missing a limb or some part of his life. In addition, he had treated Pierre badly on many occasions and harbored deep regrets for those actions. He had always intended to apologize to his brother for his past actions. But he never had the chance, thanks to the ambush on the Blood Moon that resulted in Pierre's death. Francois wanted someone to pay for taking his younger brother from him. "I am glad that he had a friend like you. Reynita used to tell me that you are one loyal son of a bitch. As I am sure you are aware, Pierre was never like me. He was the best of my family and had a bright future ahead of him. He deserved better than what happened to him on that moon. At least he had you to be there for him at the end. I heard you laid his body to rest on the gas giant Osiris."

"Yes, we did. It was something that he had wanted."

"I know. Thank you for doing that for him," Zerbe said softly.

"Is that what you wanted to say to me?" Gillis challenged. He still had the vivid memory of Zerbe causing a rumble at the wedding party of Dia Cho and Felicia Essex. Gillis still considered the actions by Zerbe that day to be uncalled for and lacking in common courtesy. Zerbe and his friends could have waited for the party to end and fight out in the streets. Poor Dia and Felicia not only had their wedding party crashed, but it had been literally crashed. And it had been done so by the man standing before Gillis.

"Partly. I have many things to atone for. I cannot tell Pierre how sorry I am for the way I treated him in life. Nor can I ask Dia and Felicia for forgiveness for my actions at their wedding. I understand if you have ill will toward me, Les. If I were in your shoes, I would not want to be working with me. All I can tell you is that I know how wrong I was in my past. Losing Pierre made me see what I was, how wrong I was. Now, here I am with a commanding officer giving me orders to do something I disagree with. My dilemma here is whether I follow or disobey my direct orders. I have orders to kill all of you and everyone inside that bar," Zerbe said loud enough for the six to hear.

Midnight growled.

BB hissed.

"I swore to follow the orders of my commanding officers when I became a Marine. But that was with the belief that my commanders would issue orders that were common sense and backed with moral authority. Killing you and these other people seems very wrong to me. All any of you have done is stand up for your basic rights, which we should all be allowed to do. I also watched, as I am certain you did, as the Royal Family fired upon a disabled space craft that had a Captain begging for mercy. That violated all the tenants of the Rules of Engagement that we were taught at the Academy and it was just damn wrong. I did quite a bit of research regarding the death of my brother on that moon. I learned that you were ambushed by Saharakaree that were under some form of mind control by some family members of the Glorious Leader. I concluded that my brother was killed by the Rosenburg family. Are my conclusions correct?"

"Yes, he was killed by the Rosenburg's. So was Porfirio and all those cadets from the other Academies. Those of us that lived, well, we were lucky to walk away from it all." Gillis nodded and paused for a moment. "I can only speculate that the Rosenburg side got over confident, they did not think we would have the internal fortitude to fight back. I held Pierre's hand in mine. I felt his blood spilling onto my tunic and saw the look of pain and hopelessness in his eyes as he passed. He was my friend, Francois. The Rosenburg's killed him."

"And they are Royals?"

"Yes they are."

Zerbe sighed, "Then I suppose that I have to break

my oath. Those bastards killed my little brother and I cannot align myself with that kind of company. No rank or position or monetary compensation could make me stand to follow their directives any further. Les, the platoon that surrounds us is under my command. Each of the men and women in my platoon has expressed their loyalty to me. Some of them lost family or friends on Chronos and the Second Fleet. I am assuming that you were planning on taking the engine room?"

"That thought had crossed our minds," Gillis admitted.

Zerbe put his arm around Gillis, "The outer hull of the station has taken some direct hits from R-5 Rockets and laser bursts. The defense soldiers have had to seal a few secondary bulkheads to protect us from explosive decompression and loss of oxygen. We will need to plan to get off of this station. It is no longer stable enough to protect us from the ravages of space. My platoon is completely loyal to me. You and your friends need to take the engine room. It is a good move. From there you can force the rest of the loyalists to the Glorious Leader to surrender. My Marines and I will simultaneously take out the weapons section so that we can repel any outside attacks."

"Are you shitting me?" Karla blurted out. She had been preparing herself to die, to be shot by some soldier with a searing hot laser blast ripping her body in half. But now the commander of the platoon that had been sent to ambush them was talking as if he was one of them. The conversation was far too good to be true.

Zerbe smiled at her, "Not at all. But a lovely lady like you should mind your language. Perhaps when this is over I can take you to bed and teach you a few things."

"I highly doubt that!" Karla felt like slapping the arrogant Marine officer.

Zerbe ignored her, "Now, Les. I watched your performance on the Blood Moon. You proved to be some form of tactical genius out there. You said that the Rosenburg's had not been ready for you to fight back. That is one way to interpret what happened on that moon. I came to another view. Your team outsmarted and out worked the enemy. Battle is not just the fight, but the planning and preparation before the conflict begins. You and your team were ready when the final battle went down. If we are all to live to see tomorrow, then we need to have a repeat performance out of you."

"I have a plan, but it does not involve fighting to hold our ground. We need to get off of this station,

Francois. It is a floating death trap. We need to get everyone off the station and flee to another location. Which brings me to my main question. How bad a shape is the Wisconsin in?"

Zerbe laughed, "You want to take the Wisconsin? That is crazy talk. Admiral Gannon is one of the most security conscious leaders in the service. Captain Ana Rendon is a cutthroat of a woman and a devious commander. I watched her have her chief engineering officer thrown out of an airlock just because he dared to debate one of her orders. She would just love to cut off your testicles, dip them in hot sauce and eat them raw. The Wisconsin MI soldiers have security systems in place that not even the best hackers can get through. The other problem is that the dark matter converter is damaged. We are not certain what happened to it, but we suspected an inside job. So if you were to take her, you would be running on the old solar-nuclear hybrid engine which might get you past several dozen AU at a lower speed. But eventually you would need to find a power source. You need a better ship, a much faster ship. Forget the Wisconsin."

"Rendon and Gannon are both Royals," Karla concluded when she heard the names.

"Correct," Zerbe nodded.

Zerbe nodded and whistled for his first two squads to join them for their instructions. He had an extra laser pistol and handed one to Mittens. "You look like a man that knows how to put this to use."

"How can you tell?" Mittens asked as he took hold of the weapon in his right hand.

"You look like a fighter if I ever saw one," Zerbe told him.

"So then what do you suggest?" Midnight asked.

"Follow him," Zerbe pointed to Gillis. "Take the engine room and my team will take the weapons section. Very simple."

"No, not so simple." Gillis sighed. If Zerbe had meant them any harm, he would have killed them already. Gillis decided to take a chance and tell Zerbe the entire truth of their destination. "My wife and friends are being forced to land on the docking area and will be arriving any minute. They are in a Raumschiff full of Clovis cadets and civilians. They will either be arrested or killed after they land on this station. We have to get to them first. That was where the six of us were headed when we ran into you."

Zerbe laughed out loud, "Six against a company of highly trained MI soldiers? Are you nuts? They would cut you down before you had time to fart. You are braver than I thought. Okay, three fronts then. That might work out well. It could divert their forces from the most important target which is the engine section. I am going to give you one of my squads to go with you. I will give another squad to help take the engine room. The last two squads will go with me and anyone you can spare to the weapons area. You hit the docking bay hard, Les. And I mean you and your friends here just light it up. The whole station will go on alert. The soldiers in the weapons section will be sent to back up those in the docking area. My team and I will be waiting in the corridor and ambush them."

"And the engine room?" Karla asked.

"My squad and your people take it. It is the least guarded area on the space craft. But be careful. Admiral Gannon and Captain Rendon are guests of the space station commander. His name is Antonin Sikorsky. He is a grandson of the Glorious Leader and he is a mean son of a bitch. His executive officer is Commander Aidan Welker, another grandchild of the magnificent leader. That's four Royals on this station. There were others but they have been killed by the people in that bar, that is why they sent me to come and take you out. You guys better be ready to kill them all." Zerbe took a breath and looked at Midnight and Ortiz. "They have some of your people hostage. But I am sure that you already knew that."

Midnight, Mittens, BB and Nappy growled at that.

"Who?" Mittens demanded.

"A couple of cat people and there is an Ortiz woman there as well," Zerbe told them. "Mean anything to you?"

Karla nodded, "They have my tia and Midnight's sister. Was there anyone else missing from your family?"

"Only my sister and her family," Midnight growled. He had hoped that his sister, her human husband and their seven children had been hiding in some safe location. The fact that they had caught her was disturbing and made the need for confrontation with the forces of the space station much more pressing. Midnight was aware of the propensity for sadistic torture of prisoners by the Royals and he hoped that he could spare his sister and his nephews that pain.

"Okay then," Zerbe nodded. "We will do all we can to liberate the prisoners but first we need to move out. You ready?"

"We are ready," Gillis motioned with his arm for Joe Ortiz and the others to come out from the bar. "Francois, this is Joe Ortiz. He owns this bar and his people are ready to fight. With your platoon we just might have a chance."

"Oh we will take the engine room that I can promise." Zerbe shook Joe's hand. "But the docking area and the weapons section are different matters altogether. They have a lot of well-trained soldiers guarding them. I wish you all luck."

"Same to you," Gillis told him. He watched as Zerbe took his two squads and some of the humans under Ortiz and the cat-human family to invade the weapons section. The second squad and the group of rebels left for the engine room. Gillis retrieved his weapons from the floor and nodded to his team of five and the eleven Marines that Zerbe left to go with him. He noticed that the squad leader, a female sergeant that had a name tag that read Kolb, was holding a laser rifle in her hand and looking up at him with the eyes of a person ready to fight.

"What is your name?" Gillis asked her.

"Sergeant Kolb."

"What is your first name?" Gillis prodded her.

"Jennifer," the woman answered. She was an average looking woman and Gillis could tell that she was in great conditioning, as was the rest of her squad members. Her Class C uniform did not allow for awards or ribbons, but the way she seemed to have no fear in her eyes indicated that Kolb had seen action before. Gillis was correct about the lady as she had been in several skirmishes over the years and had been in five different major battles in different solar systems. Her skin pigmentation was a bright pink which led Gillis to conclude she was a Cootronian. She had been assigned to serve on the science vessel *Wisconsin* as part of Zerbe's platoon against her wishes. Kolb did not like the idea of spending her time playing security guard on a ship full of computer technicians and stuffy scientists. She preferred to be on the front lines.

"Nice to meet you Jennifer," Gillis shook her hand. "We are going to take the docking area and rescue my friends. What would you suggest to be the best course of action?"

Kolb looked over at Midnight, BB, Mittens and Nappy and thought for a moment. "My squad will go in first and take up positions on the four corners of the area. You six come in about five minutes after and go high. The docking area has a massive amount of floor space to house all of the space ships that land there. The outer hull has to be opened by a control station on the offices that are on the upper level of the Docking Bay. You five will have to take it out. If you don't, the technicians that are working in the control tower will be likely to panic and open the hull and we all die when we get exposed to outer space."

"Where are the stair cases located to get to the upper control level?" Karla asked.

"The entrance to the observation tower is from the security room which is accessed only by going through a series of thick metal doors. So the best way to secure it is from the docking bay. You, um, what are you guys called?" Kolb asked Midnight.

"The humans that spliced the DNA of felines and humans together called us Kotek. We do not like that name. We prefer to be called by our birth names. I am Midnight. This is Nappy, BB and Mittens." Midnight told the sergeant.

Kolb nodded, "Well, Midnight, BB, Nappy and Mittens, we will have to use your natural acrobatic abilities to take Mister Gillis and Miss Ortiz to the upper balcony and fight to secure the watch tower. You do that and then my squad will start firing on all of the MI solders that are present on the ground level. There are fifteen of us and I estimate over a hundred enemy MI soldiers in the docking bay. We are going to be seriously outnumbered."

Gillis holstered a laser pistol into his utility belt, "Correct, but when we start firing there will be numerous civilians present that will be looking for a chance to escape. Some of them will jump in and help us. Others will just panic which will still work to our advantage. The soldiers will not know who is a combatant and who is not. But I think the MI will not expect such a bold move. The odds favor us."

"I hope you are correct," Karla said softly. She regarded faces of Gillis and the new Marines that were going into battle with them. Each of them was stolid in their facial expressions. She wondered how they could remain so calm when they were about to face death.

"Let's go," Gillis told them.

CHAPTER SEVEN

On board the *Blues City*, James Hill occupied the pilot seat, guiding the ship behind the Allen Type Fighters that had been dispatched from the space station to lead them in. Hill was dressed in a one piece white outfit with fake diamond studs and high heeled shoes. He had fancied himself as an Elvis Impersonator and would sing the songs of the music legend to himself while he flew the space craft.

Sitting next to him in the co-pilot seat was Jack Harcourt, a man with the ability to read minds or even control another person's actions by taking over their minds. He could even lure a mate to his bed by emitting scents from his pores and causing the other human to lose all control of themselves. The humans that had been involved in such a sexual encounter with a Harcourt found the experience to be one of the most intense of their lives.

Harcourt loved to fly space craft and he enjoyed hearing Hill sing. Harcourt had never heard of the man that

Hill seemed to worship. But the words and the tunes resonated with Harcourt and he wanted to know more about the man that had originally recorded them. He listened as Hill gave him a quick lecture on the life of the man he called the King and a rundown of some of his greatest songs. Hill promised Harcourt that he would give him a copy of all of his music disks provided they both survived what was about to happen when they arrived at Space Station Cy-5.

The owner of the *Blues City* was Giles Lancer, a former Space Command officer and freelance pilot. Since his retirement from the service, Lancer became a smuggler of illegal weapons and would occasionally take in passengers for a fee and let them tag along for the ride. Lancer had been widowed years ago and never remarried. He was a tall man and his voice was loud. After Bolt had made his attempt to take the ship, the security on the space station had intercepted the *Blue's City* with smaller fighter ships to force her to land. Understanding that his ship could not sustain an attack of many smaller and faster fighter ships, Lancer capitulated and agreed to the demands.

Lancer had many illegal weapons on board and he had revealed that fact to the passengers. He armed each and every one of them and ordered for them to assemble in the lower portion of the space craft where the loading dock was. It was the best point on the ship to have the room for everyone to congregate and to exit the ship quickly. Lancer waited for everyone to arrive.

Jill Mayne had a laser pistol in her right and her eyes indicated that she was bewildered by the events around her. She and her husband were simple people that were on vacation and then they found themselves caught up in the current situation. She seemed to be holding up well considering that she had just recently lost her husband in such an abrupt manner.

Daniel Choi had chosen a laser pistol as his weapon of choice. Lancer had learned from a short conversation with the young man that he had a black belt in karate and had competed in some competitions on his home planet. Choi was ready and Lancer had no doubt that the young man would rise to the occasion.

Standing next to Choi was Lucius Andolini. He had picked up a laser rifle and had loosened up the sling so that he could slide it over his right shoulder.

Two of Lucius' sisters, Giola and Venus, were standing next to him. The two girls were identical twins and had a third sister named Stella that looked exactly like them. The three women were models and cheerleaders for the Clovis City futbol, or soccer, team and had become quite famous. Their posters of them dressed in tiny bikinis or revealing outfits were selling all over planet New Edinburgh and beyond. All three of the Andolini girls were part of a five birth set. Lucius was the fourth and his identical twin brother was named Paolo. Paulo and Stella had remained on planet New Edinburgh while the other three joined up for what was supposed to be a vacation. But now it was about to be a fight to survive. Although many would not think that they were capable of self-defense, Giola and Venus were also well trained in hand to hand combat. They had been on the swim team in their high school classes and learned from their older brothers to stand up and fight when necessary.

Norman Porter was a tall and skinny eighteen year old that was deeply in love with Giola. Lancer could tell that the young man was smitten beyond words by the way Porter would look at her. Porter had decided to join the group only because he knew Giola was going. He had a look in his eyes that clearly indicated that he was ready to die fighting. Lancer watched the young man select a laser rifle and pistol from the numerous weapons lockers on the floor.

W.C. Harriak was an elderly retired miner that had

many estranged children out in the eight solar systems. He was a rough looking man, muscular and had grey hair. He had picked out a machete, a laser rifle and a laser pistol to use. Harriak had been in some fights before as mining on other planets was not a safe life style. Rival labor unions or people with money would send in hit men and hit women to kill all of the workers and take control of the mine. Harriak had to fight off several such attacks in his time and he learned through those incidents what it was like to kill others. He had no qualms about doing what was necessary to help the young kids on the ship live to see tomorrow. He had confided in Lancer that he had lived a good life, but he wanted to make sure all of the cadets on the ship had the same opportunity.

Rolf Rhinehard was a tall and muscular lad from Dresden, Germany of Old Earth. He was smart and a talented pilot. Ever since the Blue's City had left New Edinburgh, Rolf had found another married woman to have an affair with, Minxia Lu Bolt, one of Joseph Bolt's eight wives.

Seven of the eight women that were married to Bolt present. All seven were desirable and lovely in their own way. Bolt seemed to enjoy variety in his women as they were all from different ethnic backgrounds. Ever since Bolt had killed one of the passengers and failed in his attempt to take the ship, the seven women gravitated to Rolf and stayed close to him. Lancer could understand why the one named Minxia was with Rolf since she had been sleeping with him. But the others were another question. Perhaps their sister wife was their unofficial leader and they were following her. Rolf was patient with them, taking his time to teach the ladies how to operate the laser pistols. They were hanging on his every word as he instructed them how to aim and fire the weapon. All seven of the women were batting their eyelashes at Rolf and liberally pushing their bodies against him as he was instructing them on how to aim the lasers.

Doernitz sat silently on one of the metal benches against the wall, holding a laser rifle in his hands and had a laser pistol attached to his web belt that he had found and wrapped around his black trousers. He had on a dark purple sweater with the Clovis Academy logo on the front. Lancer could tell by the look in his eyes that he was in a zone, as if he were mentally ready for the conflict that awaited them.

Lila Zapata was the same age as her husband and a brilliant engineering student. She had been known to rebuild engines faster than her peers. She was a lovely lady and a bit naive. She had picked up a laser pistol and held it tight in her hands and kept looking at her husband. He would whisper words of encouragement to her which seemed to help her keep calm. Her best friend, Sophia DuBravac, sat on her other side and was also talking to her to ensure she would remain focused on the situation.

DuBravac had been born and raised in the Bordeaux area of France and was a stunning looking woman. She was not afraid of a fight and was feared by women and men alike. She was in excellent physical conditioning, had great grade marks and was smart as a whip. She spoke several languages and had a good grasp on political science. She was also experienced with the subjects of weapons and engineering.

Lancer watched as DuBravac began operating her hand held communication device and was engaging someone in dialogue. She stood up and was quite animated as she spoke. Lancer heard her speaking in French to whoever was on the receiving end of the conversation. She paced around and finally closed her device shut. She looked around and saw Lancer. She ran toward him, her eyes were wide with excitement.

"What is wrong?" Lancer asked her.

"My husband said for us to stand down. He wants us to not fight when we walk outside onto the space station docking area." She told him loudly.

Lucius heard her and he approached them, "Les does understand that they are going to arrest us, doesn't he?"

"Yes, he does. He is going to rescue us. He told me that he has joined up with a group of fighters and they are going to get us out of this mess." DuBravac spoke rapidly; her French accent was evident whenever she spoke fast.

"Well, if Les says so then that is good enough for me." Lancer responded. "We stand down. No shooting when we exit the Blue's City until Les gives us some sign to do so."

"And what if he and his army are late?" Porter piped in. "I mean, can we trust this guy? I don't even know him."

DuBravac glared in Porter's direction. Rolf knew that if Porter did not shut his mouth she would shut it for him.

"If my husband said he is going to rescue us, then he will." She had her fists ready to slug the whining cadet. She still glaring in his direction as he continued to speak.

"Really? Those people on the station are going to kill us!" Porter's voice sounded shrill.

Giola shook her head disapprovingly at Porter. She

could not believe she had just finished giving her virginity to him. She did so because she was scared of dying without ever having a man make love to her. She had wanted her first time to be special. Now the man she gave herself to was turning out to be a whiner and a coward. "Jeez, Norm! You are talking about Uncle Les. He has never let us down. What the hell is wrong with you saying things like that?"

Venus had witnessed DuBravac knock two men that were much larger than her on their butts. It had been in the bar called O'Malley's during the Blood Moon Incident. Venus pitied any man or woman that pissed DuBravac off. By the look she was giving Porter, he was about to receive an ass kicking. "Norm, you should really shut the hell up."

Porter began pacing back and forth, "They have soldiers on that station and all we have is a guy that claims to have met some people and is going to save us? We are all about to die!"

That was his last words before DuBravac punched him in the nose with her closed left fist. Porter fell on the metal floor, holding his nose and felt blood dripping down his upper lip. He could see that some of the observers were looking at him with pity, others with a look of disgust. But not one of the others lifted a hand to help him. Porter realized he was alone and that if he spoke again DuBravac was ready to make him regret it.

"You say another word and I will bust your teeth!" DuBravac growled at him. "Now get up and get a towel. You are bleeding all over Mister Lancer's floor. That is just rude."

Porter stood up without a word and began to walk away. He looked over toward Giola to see if she would follow him. To his dismay she did not. She stood with her sister next to her, both of them shaking their heads at him. He saw that both of the girls had no intention of helping him. They stood firmly with DuBravac. Porter slowly left and walked to the nearest restroom to clean the blood from his lip and chin. He knew in his heart that his emotional outburst had most likely cost him any chance of a long term relationship with Giola. He would have to work hard to better himself in her eyes so that he could win her back to his life and his bed.

The rest of the passengers of the *Blue's City* said nothing as Porter left them. His only close friend, Choi, was quiet. Choi thought that DuBravac was a little too quick to anger and probably resorted to physical confrontation too hastily. But given the amount of force she packed in her punch, Choi determined that he would allow someone else to tell her that if they were so inclined to do so. He worried for his friend, not because he had been embarrassed in front of everyone, but because his emotional state could bring risk of harm to the others. He clearly was not handling the stress of the situation well. Choi hoped that Porter would not get the rest of them killed by doing something stupid.

Unaware of the events in the lower level of the ship, pilots Hill and Harcourt were both singing a song when they saw something in the distance caused them both to stop singing. There was a large Battle Cruiser floating in space just about twenty kilometers away from the station. It looked like the ship was abandoned the way it was tilted upside down and slowly rotating in a circle.

"That is odd," Harcourt observed.

"Yes it is," Hill affirmed. "Computer, confirm is that the Wisconsin?"

"No. The ship before us is the Virginia," the computerized voice responded. "The Wisconsin is docked with the space station."

Harcourt and Hill exchanged confused glances. The *Virginia* had been slated to be decommissioned several times in the past and used as a museum for grade school students to visit. But fate had more in store for the old ship. She had been converted into a transport to fly prisoners from planetary systems to serve out their sentences on the prison planet called Cootron. The fact that it was floating in space, between solar systems, was odd. Harcourt and Hill stared at the large space craft that was listing aimlessly.

"What is a prison ship doing all the way out here?" Harcourt wondered out loud. "She was just at New Edinburgh collecting the convicts that killed our friends on the Blood Moon and during the Sandstorm Incident. They should be on their way to Cootron right now which is far west."

Hill wanted to know the answer to that question as well, "Computer, scan the Virginia for life signs."

The computer was silent for about forty seconds until it responded. "No human life signs on board the Virginia."

"None?" Hill asked.

"None. Not even a cat, sir." The computer did try at humor occasionally and always failed miserably.

Hill shrugged, "What do you think, Jack?"

"I think the prisoners broke out and escaped," Harcourt speculated. "Some of them were really pissed off at my friends when they were convicted. We should warn people right away."

Hill looked out the transparent metal windows at the

Fighter ships that were "escorting" them to the space station. "But who do we warn? We are about to become prisoners ourselves. Besides, the Virginia is an older model ship. Space pirates could have raided her. Some older ships like her have been known to have engine issues that would result in the crew having to abandon ship."

Harcourt grunted, "Let's hope we can escape and get the word out to others. The prisoners that were on that ship were dangerous people. If they escaped, then the victims could be in danger."

"I have scanned the Virginia and there is no engine damage. She is fully operational. I cannot access her computer to determine the reason for her abandonment."

Harcourt nodded as the computer reported and asked: "Can the Virginia support life?"

"Yes," came the response. "The life support systems are all fully functional."

The two men finally saw the space station in the distance, just over the upper part of the hull of the *Virginia*. There were several ships being forced to land inside the docking bay area. Hill pointed to the right of the station at the Science Cruiser *Wisconsin* that was attached to the bottom of the large space facility.

"And there is the Wisconsin," Hill said. "So we will

be facing off against the space station security and the soldiers on board the Wisconsin. I am glad I wore my best Elvis suit."

"Why is that?" Harcourt asked him.

"Cause when they kill me I will be the best dressed dead man on the space station," Hill told him. The expression on his face meant that he was not joking. Hill was a man that was ready to face his enemies and perish fighting.

Harcourt self-consciously looked himself over. He was wearing a dark green jump suit that had a zipper down the middle and numerous pockets all over. His black boots were old and scuffed. He could not recall the last time he had shined them. "And I will be the worst dressed dead man."

Hill pulled off his small headphones from his ears and looked at Harcourt with a strange look on his face.

"What now?" Harcourt sighed.

"The Second Fleet was wiped out, Jack. The Glorious Leader killed everyone."

"And?" Harcourt could tell that Hill had more to say.

"And the Glorious Leader just ordered that eleven world populations be exterminated. Old Earth is the top of the list. They are going to commit planetacide on eleven different moons and planets."

Harcourt looked out toward the Space Station Cy-5. It was growing larger and larger as they drew closer to it. "We have to do something."

"What are we going to do?" Hill challenged. "I am a retired pilot and you are a cadet. Those eleven weapons are going to vaporize over forty billion people and there isn't a damn thing you or I can do about it. We just got to try and survive our own predicament."

Harcourt closed his eyes for a few seconds as he tried to reach out with his powers to see if he could read the mind of anyone on the space station. He was not able to as they were still too far away. He opened his eyes and looked at Hill. "We can do something. If we live we can take control of either the Virginia or Wisconsin and do some damage."

Hill laughed out loud, "You are nuts, you know that?"

Harcourt shrugged, "I have been called worse."

"Look at the space station, Jack. There are several holes in the outer hull. Look over to the north-east. You see them? Look at all of those one man fighter ships out there. They are fighting to the death. How do you propose we get past those two warring factions? We don't even know which side is which. Who would we ally ourselves with?"

Harcourt nodded as he squinted his eyes to see the scorched burn marks on the outer hull of Cy-5. There were a few holes that were most likely created by R-5 Rockets or some other metal piercing explosive. Harcourt and Hill exchanged concerned looks at one another. They both realized that the station might not be a place of refuge. Hill began to think that Harcourt was correct with his idea that they should steal one of the Battle Cruisers.

The adrenaline level of the passengers on the *Blue's City* began to rise as they saw that they were about to land on the docking level of Space Station Cy-5. DuBravac hugged Lila and Jurgen and told them both that she loved them. They both told her the same. The Andolini siblings were hugging everyone, including the people they did not really know such as Harriak, Mayne and the Bolt wives.

Choi was nervous but he held his laser pistol in his right hand tightly.

The *Blue's City* slowly entered into the docking area after the protective outer hull opened for them. Hill and Harcourt could see that there were several Raumschiffs, some smaller transport ships and a few one man space ships that had already landed there and were connected to chains from the metal floor of the Docking Bay to keep the ships from drifting off in the zero gravity. Once the *Blue's City* landed, the rear outer hull of the space station would close behind them and the area would pressurize with oxygen and gravitational power so that the passengers and crew could safely step off the ship for processing.

Each of the passengers felt the ship land with a thud. Lancer cursed Hill as it was not one of the best landings that the man had completed. They could all hear the grinding noise of the outer hull shutting behind them.

"Get ready," Lancer told the others.

Hill and Harcourt joined them with Joseph and Anna Bolt in tow. The two Bolts were handcuffed together and did not make eye contact with any of the others. Mayne glared at them, her hatred for them was boiling inside her, giving her a strong desire to obtain retribution for causing the death of her husband. She wanted to shoot them both dead but was cognizant enough of the situation that revenge would have to wait.

The outer hull slammed shut. The computer alerted them that the space station oxygen and environmental controls were now stabilizing the area. After thirty seconds they were cleared to exit the *Blue's City* and enter the outer area of the space station.

Lancer ordered his on board computer to open the back ramp and the protective hull. Lila leaned into her husband closely and he instinctively put his arm around her.   "I love you Jurgey."

"I love you too," he kissed her as if it would be their last embrace.

The back doors slid open and they could see that there were several women wearing the black Class C uniforms of the MI waiting for them. All of them had laser rifles aimed at them except for one. She was a Lieutenant and she stepped forward looking the passengers over. Her name tag read Gray and she had no weapon in her hand. She smiled as she noticed that the passengers were all armed.

"Well, well, well," Lieutenant Gray said with humor in her voice. "Transportation of illegal weapons is a major felony. You will each go down for that. I suggest you drop the weapons before we have to carry out your death sentence right here and now."

As Gray was speaking, the secondary bulkheads were sliding open to reveal the larger portion of the Docking Bay. In the distance behind Gray and her soldiers were lines of other citizens that had been forced to land on the space station. They were being processed by MI soldiers. The south part of the docking area was where the Blue's City has landed. To the north was the wall where the traffic control offices were and the two balconies that were patrolled by MI snipers. The east wall was where the arriving travelers would check into the security desks and present their identification papers. On the west wall was several exits that those that had cleared their security checks could depart. It was also the only area to enter the Docking Bay to board a transport or for a citizen to retrieve their own space craft for departure.

Lancer observed a few piles of dead bodies on the metal floor; most of them had the sign of the cross branded on their cheeks. Some looked fresh and others had clearly been dead for a while. As a former soldier, Lancer recognized that each of the bodies had laser wounds on them. Most were in the abdominal area which would leave the victim in pain for many minutes before death would take them. Lancer dropped his laser pistol to the floor.

"Smart man," Gray smiled at Lancer. "How about the rest of you?"

All of the others slowly started to follow Lancer's example and discard their weapons.

"They are traitors!" Joseph Bolt screamed out loud. "They handcuffed me and my wife so that I would not be able to escape and warn you! They mean to kill the Glorious Leader!"

"That's a lie!" Venus yelled at him.

"He killed my husband!" Mayne pointed at Bolt.

Gray simply shook her head as the bickering among the passengers continued. It was not uncommon for passengers on long space flights to start to develop animosity with one another. She kept yelling at them all to drop their weapons and depart the Raumschiff. One by one, the passengers did as Gray instructed. The Andolini's stayed together as they walked down the ramp of the *Blue's City*. Jurgen and Lila were close behind them. Lucius glared at the female MI soldiers that were aiming their laser rifles at them. He wanted to curse them, but he was certain they would open fire if he did.

"When mom and dad find out about this we are so grounded," Lucius whispered to his sister Giola.

"I would say being grounded is the least of our worries," Giola responded softly.

Porter walked out and was followed by Choi. They could see the high ceilings of the Docking Bay and that there were numerous ships that were there. Choi attempted to count the number of people in line but found it to be too difficult a task to complete. He observed a squad of Marines as they walked into the area from the connecting hallway outside. They began to spilt up and go toward each corner of the Docking Bay. They were all carrying their laser rifles in their arms as if they were ready for a shootout.

DuBravac walked down the ramp with her head held high. She surveyed the activity before her. The lines of civilians were numerous. There were eleven Marines that had split up into the corners and she counted over one hundred MI soldiers. Some of them were processing the civilians. Some were walking around with weapons in their hands. They looked menacing in their black fatigues, caps and boots. She looked upward and saw the two balconies where the MI had placed snipers to keep an eye on the crowd. There were a dozen of them with laser rifles aimed downward at the crowd on each balcony for a total of twenty-four snipers. Their lasers had scopes on them to ensure accuracy. The first balcony was twenty feet off the floor and the second was forty feet up. On the highest level she observed that there was a large office with five more MI soldiers and two female technicians inside. She wondered why they would not have one way glass so that people could not see inside.

"Not very secure," she whispered to herself.

As she walked onto the floor and was directed toward one of the long lines, she could hear the secondary bulkhead beginning to close. Lancer, Harcourt and Hill were soon beside her, walking rapidly as Gray shouted threats at them. Rolf walked slowly and at one point noticed that the seven Bolt women were next to him. One of the Bolt women had a young child in her arms. Minxia was closest to him, smiling up at him when she noticed he looked at her. He said nothing for fear that the trigger happy soldiers might take his comments as some form of threat. Mayne was close behind them, acting as if she belonged to the other Bolt women.

Joseph and Anna Bolt pled their case to be released with Gray and the Lieutenant was not listening to them.

"Lieutenant, I have valuable cargo in that Raumschiff for your station Commander!" Bolt raised his voice. "I have a contract. I have papers with a bill of sale and proper security clearances from the Secretary General of planet New Edinburgh."

"Shut your mouth before I blow it off," Gray warned Bolt as she aimed a laser pistol at his right cheek. Her shift had been one of the most stressful of her military career. Gray was looking for any excuse she could find to start killing people.

Midnight Bauslaugh entered the docking area with Mittens, BB and Nappy behind him. The three hybrid feline humans found a row of narrow but long pipes on the wall that they could easily climb. The pipes led to the first and second balconies on the far west side where the dreaded snipers and the control room were located. Midnight looked at Les Gillis and Karla Ortiz as they walked in. Midnight pointed with is right hand toward the pipes. Karla and Gillis quickly walked over to them, but slow enough to avoid attracting attention. Fortunately, the snipers were surveying the ships and the crowd and were not watching the north entrance into the docking area. The soldiers that were patrolling the lower level were more concerned with the people that had landed and were being processed by the MI enlisted men and women on the east wall.

Gillis wrapped his arms around Midnight's neck and he held on as Midnight's double jointed arms and legs shifted so that he could climb up the pipes. Gillis was amazed at how quickly the muscular cat-human moved upward. He was certain it was from all the years as a traveling acrobat. Mittens followed them, climbing up another pipe just as easily with Ortiz on his back. Nappy was rapidly going upward and passed the others as he had no one on his back and could climb that much faster. Gillis prayed that the MI soldiers below did not see them.

Sergeant Kolb was waiting in the south-east portion of the Docking Bay. She had two female Marines with her. All three of them had their laser rifles ready to start firing on the MI soldiers. She had placed three Marines at the north-east corner, three at the south-west and two at the north-west. She made brief eye contact with Midnight and Gillis as they had walked in. Kolb acted nonchalant as the three Kotek's began scaling the pipes to begin the battle.

Down below, Harcourt observed what was happening. Good old Les, he thought to himself as he watched his friend hanging onto the back of the solid black Kotek. "Time to help out," Harcourt told himself.

Harcourt had previously told Hill to be ready to hold him upright as he was not sure how much energy he would expend if he tried to take control of one of the technicians. He began to concentrate on one of the men in black on the top balcony level. It was a sniper. Harcourt closed his eyes and held onto Hill's arm. He began to find his way into the brain of the sniper. Harcourt felt his mind entering the mind of the man. He was able to rapidly learn the history of the man. He could see his childhood, the faces of his parents and siblings. Within a few seconds, Harcourt learned that the sniper was a sergeant in the MI corps. His name was Christopher John Peller and he had two wives and three children back on planet New Sao Paolo. He had killed before as a sniper and Harcourt learned that the man was also a sexual predator and killer of young boys. He had molested three boys in three different solar systems and was never caught due to his multiple changes in post assignments. He strangled his victims to death after forcing them to perform oral sex at gun point. The boy's bodies were found months after Peller had left the planet where the crimes had been committed. Peller desired to kill more, but had been stationed on the space station where opportunities to commit homicide were limited. Learning those facts from the manmade killing him that much easier for Harcourt.

Hill held Harcourt upright as they walked. Hill could see that the Nappy had made it to the top balcony and soon Gillis was there with the solid black Kotek. The black and white Kotek with the Hispanic female on his back slowly crawled over the protective rails of the lower balcony.

"They are up there getting on to the balconies," Hill whispered to Harcourt.

Using his link to the mind of the sniper, Harcourt forced the sergeant turn and aim at one of his fellow snipers on the top balcony. The female sniper looked at Peller with surprise in her eyes. Harcourt's mind control forced Peller to involuntarily pull the trigger to his sniper rifle. The female sniper screamed just before her chest and back were blown open. Her body flipped backwards and the Harcourt controlled Peller continued firing his sniper rifle at the other MI soldiers on the upper balcony. The other snipers were falling. One had his head blown off, a second had her stomach and intestines spattered all over the wall behind her and a third was trying to aim at Peller but she was too slow as she was hit in the face. The back of her head exploded and her body dropped to the metal floor of the balcony. As her corpse fell, she released her laser rifle and it fell over the protective rails and plummeted forty feet to the floor below.

Gillis did not miss a beat. With his feet firmly on the balcony rail, Gillis drew the long sword from the scabbard strapped to his back and gripped the handle with his left hand. He drew the laser pistol with his right and charged toward the other MI snipers. He fired his hand laser at the cluster as he advanced and smiled, watching the Harcourt manipulated Sergeant Peller aiming downward at the MI soldiers below and began firing at them. Midnight and Nappy were charging on all fours and leaped on two MI female soldiers and began ripping out their throats with their powerful jaws and claws. They were both screaming in high pitched voices which were quickly silenced by Midnight and Nappy.

Gillis confronted one of the MI soldiers and decapitated the man with a clean swing of the sword. The body spun around with blood spurting from the jugular as the head bounced on the balcony. Gillis immediately fired his laser pistol at the MI soldier closest to the door leading to the control tower. The blast left a hole in the soldier's chest and caused his body to flip backwards over the rails and to the floor below. The door to the control tower slid open and five more MI soldiers were charging out onto to the balcony with their laser rifles in their hands. Gillis could hear the technicians inside, screaming in fear as he began firing on the five men. Gillis was able to get off six shots in rapid succession, scoring five hits. All five soldiers fell with gaping wounds in their bodies. Gillis charged into the control tower through the open door and quickly surveyed the scene before him. One technician charged at Gillis with a clipboard held over his head. Gillis shot the man in the chest. Gillis did not wait to see where the man fell as he turned quickly and decapitated another male technician that was trying to reach for the alarm. The remaining two female technicians put their hands in the air to show their attacker that they were surrendering.

Seeing no more enemy left alive on the upper balcony, Midnight and Nappy leaped from the protective rails and grabbed the bottom rail with their tails to swing themselves down onto the second balcony where they saw Karla Ortiz and Mittens wreaking havoc on the twelve snipers there. Ortiz was firing her Ak-47 machine gun mercilessly at the soldiers in black; the loud sound of the weapon seemed to startle the soldiers since laser weapons made little to no sound at all. Her first victim she hit in the upper back with four bullets and blew four holes into the top of his torso. The second was a woman and Ortiz blew off her head with three bullets, just above the chin. Mittens was on all fours, charging the nearest MI soldier. He held out his right paw with the laser pistol that Zerbe had given him and fired. The female soldier he targeted was hit in the shoulder and the blast caused her to fall to her death below. By the time the other remaining snipers were about to react and defend themselves, Midnight and Nappy were on them. Throats were slashed open and stomachs ripped out. Blood and internal organs were flowing all over the second balcony.

Mittens ran up the side of the wall and then leaped onto the last sniper and caused her to fall off the balcony. The soldier screamed as she fell to the metal floor with the black and white Kotek on top of her. Mittens bit into her throat as she screamed and tore out her larynx. Her blood was flowing down from the balcony to the floor below where the battle was now beginning in earnest.

When the Harcourt controlled Peller began firing, DuBravac seized the opportunity and ran toward one of the MI soldiers with the rank of Staff Sergeant on his collar. She slid on the floor when she was about five feet away from him, in a similar manner that a base runner in baseball would while stealing second base. She was able to take his legs out from under him and he rolled over her legs and hit the metal floor hard. The soldier dropped his weapon as DuBravac was now on top of the man. She pulled out a knife that she had hidden under her tunic and slashed his throat. Without waiting for the soldier to bleed out, DuBravac rolled on the floor toward his dropped laser rifle. She scooped it up in both hands, got into a kneeling position, and began firing on the nearest set of MI soldiers. In just under five seconds she killed three soldiers with her accurate shooting. Their bodies hit the floor and their blood was flowing.

Several civilians were screaming in fear and running in different directions. DuBravac was forced to hold her fire as many non-combatants ran in front of her line of sight. She glared at them and screamed at them to hit the floor. Some listened while others continued their panic mode and ran in no direction that seemed to make sense.

Lieutenant Gray heard the screams of the dying from behind her. She turned around and ordered the other soldiers to fight back and kill all of the civilians present. As she began to aim her laser in the direction of the three Andolini kids. Her biggest mistake was that she did not remember that W.C. Harriak had been behind her. He grabbed Clay's head in his large hands and he twisted as hard as he could. He smiled when he heard the sound of Clay's neck snap. He dropped her body to the floor and grabbed her laser pistol from her hands as she fell. He then began firing at the MI soldiers that had been standing by her side. Within a few seconds, Harriak had killed seven soldiers. The bodies were falling down on top of each other as Harriak did not wait to marvel over his handy work. He dropped to his knees and fired at some other soldiers, his laser blasts severing their legs from their bodies.

Venus, Giola and Lucius ran for cover when the firing began and had no idea that Harriak had saved their lives. The three siblings found a good safe place to hide under one of the Raumschiff space crafts near the southeast wall. They watched as Kolb and her Marines fired on the soldiers in the black uniforms from their four corners. It had been a perfect ambush. The soldiers were falling like snowflakes in a blizzard. Lucius ran from the safety of the ship and began grabbing weapons from the dead soldiers that littered the metal floor of the docking area. He collected four laser rifles and ran back toward his two sisters. Several laser blasts whizzed by his head and back as he ran. He had no idea how many shots had come close to hitting him. He slid on the ground and his momentum ended when he was next to his sisters.

"Take one and blow them away!" Lucius yelled over the sound of the firing and screams.

Venus and Giola grabbed a laser rifle each and began looking for targets. They opened fire at a group of black clad soldiers that were rushing toward the balconies where Gillis and the three cat looking people were fighting. Several of the soldiers fell dead as the Andolini siblings showered them with laser fire.

Hill noticed that several soldiers were charging in

his direction. Harcourt was in no position to fight back. Hill looked around for any of his friends and quickly realized that he and Harcourt were alone. He knew that it came down to him to protect the man. He gently set Harcourt onto the metal floor and tried to take on the cluster of soldiers rushing him. Hill got in a few good punches before three soldiers began stabbing him with their twelve inch standard issued knives. Hill screamed as he felt the metal slicing through his skin. Despite his wounds, Hill kept fighting back. He was able to get a right cross to connect the jaw of one opponent.

Lancer joined the fighting, taking on some soldiers that had charged him and he growled as he heard the cries of his longtime friend. He saw that Hill was outnumbered by the black uniformed soldiers. Lancer shoved two soldiers to the ground, broke off his current combat and ran as fast as he could to help Hill.

Rolf yelled for the seven women that were following him around to lie down. They did as he instructed. Rolf turned to face two MI soldiers. He spun around and kicked his left leg into the air. His heel connected with the jaw of the closest soldier. The soldier flew backwards and landed onto the hard floor on his back. He dropped his laser rifle when he attempted to break his fall with his hands. Rolf landed on his feet and faced the second soldier who was trying to aim his laser rifle at him. The soldier was too slow in his reaction time which gave Rolf time to grab the barrel of the rifle and rip the weapon from his hands. Rolf proceeded to smash in the soldier's skull with the stock end of the laser rifle. The first soldier was slowly getting back to his feet only to have Rolf shove the barrel of the laser rifle into his chest and pull the trigger. The soldier's back was blown out onto the metal floor.

While Rolf was engaging the two soldiers he did not see the other soldier charging at him. Fortunately for him, Minxia Lu Bolt did see the other soldier. She jumped to her feet and tripped the soldier before he reached Rolf. He turned around in time to see Minxia stab the fallen soldier in the chest with a knife she had found on the floor. Rolf smiled at her and she smiled back. Rolf then aimed his laser rifle at another group of soldiers and began firing at them. To his surprise, Minxia picked up a laser rifle and she was standing next to him firing at will.

Doernitz was able to pull his wife to a safe location behind one of the docked Allen Type Fighter ships. The canopy was open so he instructed Lila to not move before he quickly climbed inside and activated the weapons section. Using the steering column he started aiming the laser targeting system at some of the soldiers in black and fired. The laser blasts from a fighter ship were not made to just kill a life form. They were a higher caliber or potency, meant to damage machinery or metal hulls of opposing space craft. As Doernitz fired on the MI soldiers the laser blasts caused the bodies to explode. All of the soldiers he hit were virtually vaporized. Only their smoking black boots remained.

Choi and Porter were able to retrieve weapons from some of the fallen soldiers. Both of the young cadets kneeled down, back to back, and began firing laser rifles at the MI soldiers. Neither man said a word as they kept firing and firing. Neither cadet showed any mercy as they aimed at the heads and torsos of their targets.

Joseph Bolt looked at his wife Anna and told her that they should make a run for it. She agreed and the two decided to make it back to the *Blue's City* and steal it. Bolt had valuable merchandise on that ship and needed it to complete his contractual obligations with the buyers on the space station. They got about ten feet and then stopped when they saw Mayne standing in front of them with a laser pistol in her right hand. She had rage all over her face.

"You killed my husband!" Mayne screamed over

the sounds of the laser fire and the dying. Her hand was trembling as she aimed the laser at Bolt. She had never killed a person before. The desire for revenge was enough to override her fear of pulling the trigger.

"Look, I am sorry about that. But I have lots of money on the Blue's City. Let me get it and we can work out some form of compensation." Bolt's voice was stammering as he pleaded for his life.

"Fuck your money!" Mayne yelled and pulled the trigger twice.

Bolt screamed as his chest and abdomen were blown open by the laser blasts. He was dead before he hit the floor. Anna Bolt tried to run away but Mayne fired at her legs. Anna Bolt screamed as she felt her left leg being severed just above the knee. Her right leg was hit just above the ankle. She slide to the metal floor face first and was crying in agony. Mayne walked by Anna Bolt and spit on her.

"Kill me, please." Anna Bolt said to her as she reached down at her wounds. For some reason she thought that she had not been shot. There was no blood pumping out from the wounds as she would have expected. Her plea for death was solely based on the fact that she had allied herself with Joe Bolt and that gamble had failed. Death would be preferable than a trial or facing the Andolini girls that would possibly treat her harshly.

Mayne smiled and aimed the laser pistol at her head, "My pleasure." She pulled the trigger and ended what she believed to be Anna Bolt's suffering.

Harcourt was lying on the floor without protection as Lancer and Hill were fighting with a group of other soldiers. The two men were outnumbered. Harcourt concentrated and forced Sergeant Peller to drop his sniper rifle and jump from the balcony. Harcourt released his mind control on Peller so that he would be able to have full consciousness as he fell the forty feet to his death. Peller impacted the metal floor and several of his bones cracked on impact. He struggled to try and cry for help and took about five minutes of labored breathing before he finally died.

Harcourt found a laser pistol and began aiming it at the cluster of soldiers attacking Hill and Lancer. He fired a few shots and helped even the odds for the men. Harcourt smiled when he saw Harriak rush in and help Lancer. The two older men proved that age did not matter in a hand to hand fight as they dispatched the much younger MI soldiers with little effort.

In the control tower, Gillis pointed his blade at the

two female technicians. The blade was dripping with fresh blood and Gillis was certain that the two civilian women were intimidated by the sight.

"What are your names?" Gillis demanded.

One of the girls slowly looked him in the eyes, "I am Sapai Hu. Her name is Dainia Mills. We are just computer technicians. Please, sir, we do not have any weapons on us. We are not soldiers."

Gillis cocked his head sideways as he heard her accent, "You are from Old Earth?"

"Cambodia," Hu confirmed. "Dainia is from New Sao Paolo."

"Can you eliminate the security access codes to the outer doors to the control tower?"

"Yes," Hu nodded. "It won't be easy. But yes, I can do it."

"Can you please do so?" Gillis lowered the sword to his side. "I promise we are not here to hurt you."

"Bull shit," Mills said as she looked at the other dead in the room and on the balcony.

"We only fight soldiers," Gillis told them. "You two are civilian techs. We are not here for you. In fact we are going to try and save all of you. This station is a floating death trap and we all need to work together to get off of it.

The rebels on Robert Andrews Moon are sending more small fighter ships to take this station out to eliminate the threat that they believe exists here. There is a science cruiser docked to this station and we mean to take it, if force if need be. It is our best hope to escape alive. And I mean to take all of us, even the prisoners in the Tank. We plan on leaving this station with every single person we can carry. Can you help us?"

Hu and Mills nodded affirmatively.

"You were that guy on the Blood Moon," Mills blurted out.

Gillis gave her a quick nod affirming that he had been there.

"You are a real live hero," Mills said. "I never thought I would meet a real hero before. I watched every moment of that battle. You gave that famous speech and fought against all those odds. You gave people hope. I believe you and will help you in every way I can."

Before he could respond, Gillis heard a banging noise on the balcony behind him. He looked over his shoulder and saw Mittens approaching with Karla Ortiz.

"All of the MI soldiers are dead," Karla reported proudly.

"Good," Gillis smiled. "I think these two girls are

willing to help us. I am going to find my wife."

Sapai Hu smiled and began to type commands on her type pad to do as the handsome man with the sword had instructed her to do. Gillis left the four of them alone and ran to the pipes that the three Kotek's had climbed up in the beginning. He sheathed his sword and jumped from the balcony to the pipe and wrapped his arms around it. He slid down until his feet hit the ground. He turned and began looking around the blood stained floor that was littered with dead bodies.

He did not see his wife around. "Sophia! Sophia!" He called out urgently as he ran through the crowds of the survivors. He passed the Andolini kids standing up from their safe hiding place. They smiled when they saw uncle Les.

Leaning over an injured woman, DuBravac heard her husband calling out for her. She stood up and ran toward his voice. "Les! I am over here!"

They saw each other from across the body riddled floor. They ran toward each other and fell into each other's arms after what felt like an eternity to them both. They began kissing passionately, holding each other tight. Words could not describe the joy they both felt at being reunited.

"Je t'aime ma cherie," Gillis told her in between

kisses. He could smell the floral aroma of her perfume as he held her. He had missed that pleasant smell as much as he did holding her and the taste of her lips.

"Je t'aime pour toujours," DuBravac responded as she kissed him passionately.

They kissed some more.

The Andolini siblings smiled as they watched.

"What I would give to have a man love me like that," Giola said to her two siblings.

"Ditto," Venus nodded in agreement.

Sergeant Kolb ordered her squad form up. One of her Marines had been killed in the battle. Kolb knelt over the body of her fallen squad member and pushed her eyelids closed. All in all, they had been lucky that they only lost one soldier in that they had been fighting against huge odds.

Harcourt sat up, gasping for air and feeling drained of all of his strength. Using his powers of mind control was difficult for him to do, but it had been for a good cause. Around the room and saw Lancer and Harriak kneeling over the body of James Hill. Hill's white Elvis suit was drenched in blood from the numerous knife wounds he had sustained. Harcourt felt badly as he had grown to like the man.

"We had a good run, my old friend." Lancer said softly as he held Hill's hand in his. Hill had been his best friend since the service and that friendship had continued as they became freelance pilots. They had shared hundreds of adventures over many years and no matter the danger, Hill never abandoned Lancer. "If there are Gods out there, I hope that they take good care of you. I will miss you."

Harriak found a jacket from a dead MI soldier and laid it over Hill's face. "He was a good man."

Lancer nodded, "He was the best."

Porter and Choi stood and watched as several nurses and doctors were treating the wounded. Mayne was smiling at them, still holding the laser pistol that she had used to avenge her husband with. Porter was more concerned with locating Giola. When he saw her with her two siblings, he ran to her and tried to give her a hug and a kiss. She accepted the hug but turned her head aside when he tried to kiss her lips. He had to settle for a kiss on her cheek.

Giola's refusal to kiss him made Porter angry. He did his best to hide his feelings as he was certain others were watching. He released Giola and tried to look in her eyes but she would not make eye contact with him. Porter slowly backed away from her and shook his head in confusion. Just a few hours earlier she had let him make love to her. It had been the answer to all of his prayers. But now she was giving him a cold shoulder. He did not understand why she would treat him in such a manner. He walked away from her without saying a word.

Venus noticed the odd exchange between them. She wondered what her twin sister had done to cause Porter to react in such a manner.

Lucius had not caught on to the short emotional scene as he was busy speaking to Rolf and the seven Bolt wives.

Jurgen and Lila approached Les and Sophia, exchanging hugs with one another.

"How badly were we hurt?" Gillis asked.

"We lost James Hill," Jurgen pointed over where Lancer, Harriak and Harcourt were kneeling. "I think one of your Marines was killed on the north-west wall. Several dozen civilian were killed or injured. Looks like we were lucky."

"Or damn good!" DuBravac looked at her husband with pride.

"It's not over yet," he warned them.

"What is next?" Lila asked.

Gillis looked at her, "Well Lila, I have another group attacking the engine room right now. I think the three of you would be very helpful in that area."

"You want us to shut off the oxygen regeneration machines to the rest of the Station?" Lila speculated.

Gillis laughed and looked at Jurgen, "How did you and I get the two smartest and beautiful women in the eight solar systems?"

He shrugged, "Our personalities?"

DuBravac took her husband in her arms and kissed him, "That and a whole lot of other things."

"Well, we can have this discussion later," he told his wife. "Right now we need to get out there and help some other friends of mine. We also need to organize everyone here."

"What have you got in mind, Les?" Lila asked.

Gillis motioned for the others to follow him. Gillis noticed that about thirty injured civilians were leaning against the west wall and were being treated by two doctors and some nurses. He walked quickly toward them.

One of the doctors saw them approaching and stood up, "Are you the one responsible for this massacre?"

"Yes and no," Gillis told him. "We had to attack and take this section otherwise most of you would have been either arrested or shot dead. There are over three hundred prisoners in the Tank and you saw the dead bodies of all the Christians when you arrived. Had we failed to act, all of you would have been dead or incarcerated. We had no choice."

The doctor nodded at that, recalling the piles of dead bodies that were left on the cold metal floor to rot. "Okay, so I did see the dead when I arrived. But now we have more dead due to your sneak attack."

"You have many more that are alive. I assure you that they were all going to either be arrested or killed by the commanders of this station. There is a civil war breaking out and the Royal Family has taken a posture of kill anyone and worry about their loyalty later." Gillis pointed over to the clusters of civilians that were watching their every move.

"They are all scared to death," the doctor observed.

"Agreed. We hope that we can get all of them to a safer location. What is your name?" Gillis asked him.

"LaMarcus Redd Jones, M.D., at your service. Call me Mark, all my friends call me that." He shook Gillis' hand and then the others. He smiled at Sophia and Lila as they shook his hand.

"Well, Mark, this is the deal. There is a Science Cruiser out there," Gillis pointed upwards. "And there are at least a dozen Raumschiff and other transports in here. I need you and your nurses to load the injured up and get them into one of the ships and continue treating them. My plan is to get everyone safely off this station."

DuBravac raised her eyebrow at her husband as she saw that two of the cat people were approaching. Gillis was the first to give his last dollar to another person in need. The tone of his voice indicated that he was anticipating rescuing more people that had not been along for the ride on Lancer's ship. "Who do you mean as everyone?"

Gillis gave her a smile, "I mean every one and that includes all of the prisoners in the Tank. All of these civilians here will have to start boarding these transports. I have several other friends that are probably invading the engine room and weapons section as we speak. Once they succeed with those missions, need to get off this station. We are taking everyone with us."

"And where would we all go?" Doctor Jones asked.

"Somewhere very safe. There is a moon in close proximity that is populated with rebellious forces. They will take us in. If not them then we can take flight to either New Berlin or New Quebec as those planets seem to be willing to stand up for freedom." Gillis turned his attention toward Midnight and Nappy. Both of them were covered in the blood of the soldiers that they had mangled during the battle. Nappy had a laser rifle in his hands while Midnight was still unarmed.

"I just spoke to your friend Jack," Nappy told them. "He said the he saw the Battle Cruiser Virginia just a few kilometers from this station. He said it was abandoned."

"I left Mittens up in the control tower with the Ortiz woman just in case more MI show up. If you are still planning on everyone going then we need pilots to get all of these ships ready. How many pilots do we have?" Midnight spoke with an occasional growl in his voice.

Gillis looked around the room, "Lancer, Jurgen, Rolf, Jack and Lucius. That leaves us with five pilots."

"Norman is also in the astronaut program but he is still in his first semester. That makes six. We are going to need a lot more pilots than that to get what, about four or five hundred people off this station?" Doernitz stated the obvious.

"Au garde-a-vous! Attention! Achtung! Atencion!" DuBravac surprised the men as she began yelling at the civilians. Several of them looked in her direction. She had been listening to her husband, Doernitz and the Bauslaugh's and decided to help them out with the problem at hand. She had always been the type of person that preferred taking action as opposed to talking. "Attention! I need all of you with astronaut experience to step forward! Everyone! Anyone that has flown a space craft before step forward!"

Lancer and Rolf joined the group and waited as they watched others from the clusters of civilians join them. Eighteen civilians walked over and stopped in front of DuBravac. Midnight and Nappy smiled, their sharp fangs showing, as the pilots began to gather round her.

"You all have flying experience?" She asked them.

Some answered affirmatively, others just nodded their heads. She counted them and added their number to the pilots that they already had assembled.

"Twenty-four pilots," DuBravac smiled at her husband.

"Twenty-five," Nappy raised his furry arm up. "I can also fly ships. So you have twenty-five and many of my cousins can fly also."

"So can some of the Ortiz family," Midnight added. "We need to go round them all up. We will need all the pilots we can get if we are going to take two Battle Cruisers."

"Who said we are going to do that?" Gillis asked.

"Your eyes did when we told you about the Virginia," Midnight answered quickly with a smile on his face. "Part of our acrobatic touring act is to tell what people are thinking by the expressions on their faces. Now, who stays behind and who is going to the engine section? We need to move it before the grrrrr MI soldiers mobilize and strike back at us."

Gillis put his hand on Midnight's shoulder. "Yes, my friend. We certainly do need to get on with the fight. We leave most of the pilots here, along with Harriak, the civilians and the medical crew. They get all of the wounded on board some of the Raumschiff's while we are away. Sophia, tell the others to collect the weapons from the dead MI soldiers. Sergeant Kolb!"

"Yes sir!" Kolb was already standing behind Gillis, ready for more action.

"Are you prepared to guard this location?"

"We should be going with you," Kolb said boldly.

"I need you to protect these civilians. I have Midnight and Mittens and several good fighters here to follow with me. Besides, with any luck, Joe Ortiz has already secured the engine room and Zerbe has the weapons section."

Lila held up a black backpack that she found on the floor. She had unzipped it and inspected the contents. "Les, Sophia. Look at this. Magnetic scanners which are some new models from the Brackenridge Corporation and there are some old school magnetic explosive devices. We can use these."

"What are you thinking, Lila?" DuBravac asked.

"We can use them to make sure no one else can use the engine room," she responded and smiled at her husband. "We place them in strategic locations in the engine room so that if we have to detonate them it would take repair technicians months to fix the damages."

"You see why I married her?" Doernitz hugged her.

DuBravac smiled, "So her nice ass had nothing to do with it?"

Doernitz laughed at that, "Well, that and her dimples and pretty eyes."

Zapata kissed her husband playfully.

Suddenly, the space station rocked violently to the left. Everyone except the feline-human hybrids lost their balance. Unbeknownst to them, there was a tragedy that had occurred on one of the wheels around the space station. Several of the rebel fighter ships had been engaged against the smaller space craft from the Wisconsin. During the melee between the warring factions, one of the Allen Fighters was hit by a laser burst and the pilot lost control of her ship. It spun left to right and impacted the hull of the space station wheel. Upon the collision of space craft on transparent metal, the ship and its' R-5 Rockets exploded, causing a rupture in the outer hull. The metal was breached and the oxygen was sucked out into space.

The area was a big attraction for tourists due to the anomaly in space just about two kilometers from the station. There was a cascade of green, orange, yellow, red white and other mixes of colors that were the remnants of an ancient battle. The legends from the Akarzdamedian culture stated that several hundred years earlier, they had fought a decisive battle against a powerful alien race known as the ZjNozia. Thousands of war ships clashed in that spot and battled for several Earth days to determine which species would control three solar systems. The Akarzdamedians won the war and punished the ZjNozia by annihilating their entire culture. The Akarzdamedians took the ZjNozia solar system after the battle and committed genocide on her life forms. But the electromagnetic and metallic remains from the battle remained.

When the Glorious Leader conquered the Akarzdamedians, he learned that the area of space was considered a death trap. The normal functioning of sensors that were utilized would not operate properly, sometimes causing space craft to lose their navigational and directional abilities. There had been rumors that the center of the colorful cascade was a wormhole that had swallowed up over a hundred missing space craft. The Glorious Leader did not believe in such fairy tales and in defiance of the Akarzdamedian legends, ordered that Cy-5 be constructed in close proximity to the anomaly.

The wheel was an area that also housed many civilians and soldiers in hotels and barracks. The force of the explosive decompression swept the men, women and children that were walking around the stores, food court and sightseeing ramps out into space. The wail of the sound of the rapid loss of air drowned out their screams of terror. The secondary bulkheads eventually sealed off the area. But over three hundred lives were lost before that occurred.

"What the Hades was that?" Venus demanded as she struggled to regain her footing.

"The space station suffered a direct hit!" Lancer responded as he stood. "Those idiot pilots are going to get us all killed!"

"We have space ships. We should leave!" Porter urged.

Giola rolled her eyes with disgust at Porter's suggestion that they flee.

"No," Gillis vetoed the idea of fleeing. "We would

fly right out into the middle of a war zone. And there are too many innocent people here that we have to save. We all leave together."

"Then let's get on with it," Doernitz urged as he checked his laser pistol charge level.

CHAPTER EIGHT

Zerbe led his squad of Marines, several of the Kotek's and civilians from the bar Dos Gueros Muertos to the entrance of the Weapons Section. The Weapons Section was perhaps the largest of the actual military controlled areas of the Space Station. It was located on Level Three and extended around the entire ring of the station. The purpose was so that the station defenses could guard the entire perimeter and there would be no blind spots for the enemy to gain an advantage in an attack. The outer defenses of the station consisted of the typical armor piercing rockets, laser canons, magnetic space mines, laser batteries and concussion missiles that would explode in a certain area of space with the intent of causing any approaching enemy to react to the shock waves that the explosion created.

The front entrance to the weapons area would be heavily guarded. It had a thirty foot wide doorway that was twenty feet high. Zerbe had armed several of the civilians with thermite grenades and laser pistols to go along with their crude twentieth century weapons. The hallway leading to the entrance was twenty feet wide of transparent metal and was patrolled by MI soldiers. Zerbe decided to split up his team to synchronize their entry onto level four from the eight different stairwells. He placed the feline-human named Luna in charge of one team, Junior Ortiz in charge of another, Sergeant Brannigan took the third team, Dracula the fourth team, Panther the fifth, Amy Ortiz the sixth, Lance Corporal Kim the seventh and Zerbe took the eighth team.

The multiple stairwell entrances were not the only obstacle in taking the weapons area. The middle ring of the space station was about three miles long. That meant that the soldiers and technicians had three miles worth of distance to work and thus would be difficult to apprehend all of them quickly. Zerbe had studied tactics in raiding a weapons area and he knew that the task was going to cost the lives of several of his group.

Zerbe led twelve individuals up the stairs. All of the teams had been instructed that they attack at exactly eleven p.m. That gave them just five minutes to get into position. Zerbe had three Kotek's with him named Snowflake,

Wolvie and Blu. Wolvie was a medium sized male, solid black with thick fur and a bushy tail. Snowflake was a little bigger than Wolvie and he had solid white fur with blue eyes. Blu was their cousin and she was dark but her fur had a tint of blue to it. She was one of the main acrobat performers for the family. Each of the Koteks held laser pistols in their hands. Zerbe tried not to watch when the three dropped down on all fours as their double jointed bone structure shifted so they could charge like a lion or a cheetah. The process they went through to go from walking upright to walking more cat-like just did not sit well with the Marine Corps Lieutenant.

"I can smell them out there," Blu said softly. "They are afraid. Maybe that explosion we felt earlier has tested their mettle."

"Or one of the other teams has attacked," Zerbe added. He had read that the Kotek race had many of the attributes of the cat predators. They could smell fear and possessed other instincts such as enhanced eye sight. Zerbe noticed that Blu was smiling at him.

"What is it?" Zerbe whispered to her.

"I smell you, too. You really need a mate. You want to breed."

Zerbe smiled back at her, "You don't need to smell

me to know that. I am always on the prowl for a woman."

"Have you ever been with one of us?" Blu whispered playfully to him.

"Is that even possible?" Zerbe was curious about that. Blu was attractive but with her coat of fur he wasn't certain if he could get aroused enough to make love to her.

"Yes, we do it all the time." Blu assured him. "We are more human than feline. You and me together, I think we could make beautiful litters together."

"You mean children?"

"We call it litters because we never have just one. The norm for us is three or more children in each birthing cycle. I could provide you with instant offspring. A handsome man with your muscular body, you would make a fine breeding partner. Ah. Eleven o'clock is approaching and the soldiers in the hallway are in disarray. Many of them are trying to leave to go somewhere else."

Zerbe motioned with his head to the civilians in the stairwell, "Get ready."

Sergeant First Class Zeman was at the rear of the group. Zerbe had instructed her to take command if anything happened to him. She was a stocky woman with a large nose due to having it broken if one too many fights. She held her laser rifle with the barrel pointing upward. She nodded to Zerbe that she was ready.

At eleven o'clock, Zerbe charged out of the stairwell with Wolvie and Blu next to him. Blu ran quickly passed Zerbe and charged an MI Corporal that was standing near the safety rails of the walkway. Blu leaped from her four legs onto the back of the soldier and knocked him over the rail. He screamed as he fell to his death.

Zerbe was right behind her, firing his laser at several soldiers further down the hallway. They had not been expecting the attack as their information was that a group of rebels were attacking the docking area. Zerbe's aim was perfect. Both shots hit the soldiers in the center of their heads, their skulls split open and their bodies pitched backward to the metal floor.

Wolvie leaped onto another soldier and bit into her neck with his sharp fangs. The soldier cried out in terror as her throat was ripped open.

Snowflake leaped on top of another unfortunate soldier, a female weapons officer. She screamed as Snowflake ripped open her stomach area with the claws of his back legs.

The other seven teams charged out of their assigned stairwell and adding to the casualties among the weapons staff. Dracula was doing the most damage as he threw two weapons technicians over the protective rails and slashed another across the throat with his left arm.

Laser fire filled the hallways, taking lives on both sides of the battle. Zerbe felt the tear of his uniform next to his right shoulder from a near miss laser shot. Just a quarter of an inch closer and Zerbe would have lost his arm. The screams of the fallen were echoing off of the metal walls.

Zerbe pressed his advantage into the main entrance of the weapons section. He dived into the large area through the thirty foot wide doorway and slid on his stomach, firing his laser at the workers inside. He aimed for the uniformed soldiers and tried his best to avoid hitting the civilian technicians. The weapons section was set up with two balconies and there were numerous weapons officers on duty. They had heard the screams coming from the outer walkway and were ready. They had weapons drawn and fired back. Zerbe cursed and rolled to his right as laser blasts rained around him.

Zeman led large number of civilians and Koteks into the section and began firing at the upper balconies. Junior Ortiz came in and saw that Zerbe was lying on the floor firing upwards. Junior was about to say something when his head exploded. The headless body of Junior Ortiz fell sideways to the metal floor. Another civilian with the sign of the cross tattooed on her left cheek died when a laser blast ripped through her stomach and exploded out her back.

Blu, Snowflake and Wolvie acted swiftly, rapidly climbing up the pipes and stairs to attack the snipers above. One of the weapons officers pulled out a thermite grenade pressed the detonation button and dropped it down to the lower level. It exploded and three of the civilian rebels were incinerated in the hot flames. The same weapons officer dropped a second thermite device to the floor. Zeman instinctively leaped on top of the grenade and wrapped her body around it. When it exploded she did not even scream. When the flames subsided there was nothing remaining of her.

Wolvie cried out in pain when he was hit on his upper right arm by a laser blast and he fell to the metal floor. He made a whining noise as he rolled around on the metal floor in pain. Snowflake reached the soldier that had shot his brother and ripped her stomach open with two slashes of his upper claws. The soldier dropped her rifle and fell backwards, holding her stomach as if that would somehow stop the bleeding. Snowflake charged another sniper and shoved her over the railings. He pounced on another sniper, slashing her face and neck with two rapid swings of his front paws.

Dracula and other Kotek fighters rapidly ascended the walls and soon overwhelmed the rest of the soldiers, pitching their mutilated bodies to the floor below. Zerbe leaped up onto his feet again and fired his laser at several soldiers that refused to lay down their arms. The civilian technicians were on their knees, some were crying and others begging for mercy.

Zerbe directed the remainder of his two squads to take over the weapons controls.

"Seal the door!" Zerbe instructed one of his Lance Corporals.

There were sounds of laser fire and screams of the dying in the distance. Zerbe motioned for two Marines to go right and two others to go left down the three mile long hallway to assist the others.

Zerbe turned around and saw that several of the Kotek's were tending to Wolvie's injured paw. He was whining in pain. There were a few of the civilians that had been injured and were sitting on the floor, holding their wounds. Two of the people had abdominal wounds and Zerbe knew they would not live long. But when he saw Blu lying on the floor moaning in pain he felt sick to his stomach.

Zerbe ran to Blu's side and saw that she had been shot in the stomach. She was crying and making a deep moaning sound due to the pain she was experiencing and Snowflake was comforting her by licking her forehead.

Blu saw Zerbe kneel down next to her. "I would have given you wonderful children," she said with a weak voice.

"I know you would have," Zerbe took her hand. He had never lost a soldier in a combat situation. Today he had lost several. He grinded his teeth together as he watched Blu slip into death. He felt numb. He had grown to like her in the short time he had to interact with her.

She took her last breath and went limp. Snowflake let out a sad cry as he watched his cousin die. Zerbe stood back and felt a lump in his throat as Snowflake began to nudge Blu's body with his nose and was making a strange noise that was clearly motivated by grief. He had heard that the feline-human race were incapable of feelings as they were part animal. Zerbe found out that the feline-human hybrids were quite possible more compassionate and loving than regular humans. In addition, they were capable of being good and loyal friends.

Amy Ortiz and two of the civilian rebels were already on the upper balcony checking out the operational capacity of the laser canons and other long range defenses. Ortiz seemed to be oblivious regarding the fact that her brother had been killed in the raid. Zerbe looked at Dracula who was standing over Blu's corpse and holding hands with some of the other Kotek's as they were praying in some tongue that was full of meows.

Some of the other Kotek's were tending to Wolvie's injured arm. Luna was bandaging the wound while Panther was licking his forehead in the same manner Snowflake had done for Blu.

"Wolvie, are you going to be okay?" Zerbe asked.

He nodded. Zerbe could see tears of pain in Wolvie's eyes. Or perhaps they were tears that he had from the emotional turmoil he felt from losing Blu.

"Lieutenant!" Amy Ortiz yelled down at him. "We have reset all of the passwords to the section. We now have complete control of all the weapons!"

Zerbe smiled, "Good. But at what cost?" He looked over at the burn mark where his platoon sergeant dived on top of the thermite grenade to save others. It was a victory, but not without tears.

CHAPTER NINE

Joe Ortiz had led the team to take the engine room and by default the life supports section that was located in the same section. To his shock, they met no resistance. There were no soldiers present at all and the twelve civilian engineering technicians surrendered without incident. Ortiz directed his daughters and the Kotek's to begin to take over the seats and operate the machinery. The twelve captured technicians were placed in the center of the engineering section and ordered to sit as they waited for the next commands from Gillis.

The stress level of the occupants of the Command Station of Cy-5 was high. They had been watching on several view screens as the docking area, the engine room and their weapons section had been overrun by lesser trained and poorly armed opponents. The situation was unacceptable to the commanders of the station as well as the top officers from the Science Cruiser *Wisconsin*. They watched with anger as their engineering staff failed to put up a fight as the traitors attacked. They showed little to no sympathy as all of the loyal MI soldiers fought and died in the docking area. They were disturbed by the fall of their staff in the weapons section.

Space Command Admiral Malcolm Gannon was mostly concerned about the loss of the weapons station. Space Station Cy-5 was on the edge of the solar system of the binary stars that heated Sikorsky's Planet. The station was a lay-over post for travelers that had the intent of entering the system or for those that needed supplies on their way to another star system. The closest habitable world to the space station was a moon named after a human hero of antiquity, Robert Andrews. That moon had recently declared independence from the government of the United Nations of the Eight Solar Systems and the elected Secretary General for the past two hundred years, Vladimir Sikorsky.

Gannon had arrived on the space station by way of the *Wisconsin*. Gannon had been appointed Admiral of a fleet of five large ships that were primarily used to chart the outer galaxies for other possible worlds to conquer. On her last mission, the dark matter converter on the *Wisconsin* malfunctioned. Gannon determined that the ship should abandon the mission and return to the eight solar systems for repairs. He left Captain Carol Ruiz of the Science Cruiser *Colorado* in command of the four remaining space craft as the *Wisconsin* and her crew began their trip back to the solar systems controlled by humanity. Without the dark matter converter, the *Wisconsin* had to rely on solar and nuclear power for the flight.

While on the flight back, Gannon had kept informed of the current events around the entire eight solar systems. Several planets had erupted into civil disobedience after the events on the Moon orbiting planet Semiramis.

The first of the numerous satellites to overthrow the Sikorsky run government was a moon orbiting a gas giant planet called Osiris. Vladimir Sikorsky had been ready for such an uprising. He had funded a professor and some of the best minds in weaponry, metallurgy, nuclear power and military tactics to create weapons of mass destruction so powerful that the rest of humanity would grovel with fear. The moon named Chronos was the first to suffer the wrath of Sikorsky. One of the deadly weapons that had been created was named Red Javelin and it was used on the population of Chronos. The weapon killed all living humans there in minutes after it had been detonated.

And the world watched.

Vladimir Sikorsky took credit for the atrocity and most of humanity reacted with fear of the assured destruction that would find them if they dared fight for independence.

But others were not afraid. The brave astronauts and soldiers of the Second Fleet of Battle Cruisers attempted to force Vladimir Sikorsky to step down and surrender power by instituting a blockade of the home planet named Sikorsky's Planet. The attempt failed and all of the Second Fleet was annihilated with armor piercing nuclear warheads fired by the First Fleet.

Before the destruction of the Second Fleet, other worlds began to rebel. Assassins were dispatched to eliminate the leaders. But they were too numerous. So Sikorsky determined that the easiest way to end the unrest was to use more Red Javelins to wipe them all out. Fourteen billion men, women and children were going to experience an agonizing death. By that point in time, the *Wisconsin* had already docked with Space Station Cy-5 and Admiral Malcolm Gannon was invited to spend the time needed for the repairs to the space craft with his family members on the station.

Gannon accepted and brought over all of the crew of the *Wisconsin* save the engineering officers and technicians so that they could replace the defective parts. Gannon found that the station was suffering the same unrest just as many of the planets and moons. There were rebels on the base and they were fighting to take the station. Losing the engine section was devastating and to make matters worse for the Sikorsky controlled government was that seven pilots had sacrificed themselves to destroy the Red Javelin weapons that had been launched to destroy Old Earth and the other treasonous planets. The explosion that resulted was the most devastating that humanity had ever seen.

Gannon and the command staff of the station had lost contact with Sikorsky's Planet and the First Fleet just after the destruction of the Red Javelins. With the nearby moon under the control of the freedom movement, the space station was now vulnerable.

Malcolm Gannon looked like he was about thirty but in reality he was one hundred thirty-two years old. As all of the members of the Royal Family had done, he had used the bodies of young women to stay young. He took livers, kidneys, hearts, lungs, skin and other organs to maintain his health and youthful appearance. He had trained as an astronaut and became an accomplished pilot. As the decades passed, Gannon became an expert in hand to hand combat, weapons, stellar mapping, history and politics. He had married over a dozen women in his lifetime and sired many sons and daughters. His offspring had all gone in different directions with their lives. Some had gone into military service, others pursued lives in academia or the sciences and others were captains of industry.

Gannon looked upon the other top ranking officers that were with him on the space station command station. Many of them were also descendants of Vladimir Sikorsky and they were equally concerned with their dilemma.

Captain Ana Rendon of the Science Cruiser *Wisconsin* was a member of the Royal Family as was Gannon. Rendon was sixty-one years old, widowed and had eight children. Each of her children had been forced to become pilots in the Space Command as their mother had. She had started her military service late in life which was why she had not yet made the rank of Admiral. She had grey hair and wrinkles around her eyes and lips. Her dark eyes looked tired as she watched the attack on the viewing screens on the tri-level, rectangular shaped command station. She cursed as she saw the weapons room fall so easily and to so few. Her hope was to return to the Wisconsin and take her back to the rest of the Science

Fleet. But with the number of planets falling to secession, she was all too aware that she would have to lead her Science Cruiser into battle sooner than later.

Space Station Cy-5 commander Captain Antonin Sikorsky was a grandson of the Glorious Leader. He was eighty years old and looked as if he was still in his late twenties. He had been all too willing to take the body parts of kidnaped young women to extend his life. He was just under seven feet tall, had dark hair and dark eyes with a slender build. He had started his military service as a Space Command astronaut and learned military tactics and studied advanced weaponry in his spare time. He had twelve wives during his lifetime, half that were deceased and the other half lived on Sikorsky's Planet. He had thirty-seven children, mostly girls, that were varying in age from forty-five as the oldest to twenty-one as the youngest. Some of his children went into the service, others chose other professions. He preferred the quiet and unassuming role as a commander of a space station as it required little effort and kept his stress level down. But now his mind was racing as he considered many options as he watched three of the most important section of his space station fall to enemy hands. He was angry at Gannon and Rendon for bringing their soldiers onto his station, especially the platoon under the command of the man named Zerbe. He blamed them for the three levels of the station falling into the hands of the peasant rebels. If it were not for Zerbe and his platoon, Sikorsky was certain the humans and Koteks would have failed in all three raids. With Zerbe, the advantage had switched to the side of the rebels.

His executive officer is Commander Aidan Welker, another grandchild of Sikorsky. Welker was one of the thirteen sons of the famous General Rock Murdock and had inherited many of his looks. He was muscular and had blonde hair and blue eyes. Welker was fifty years old and had died once in a small skirmish on planet Athena. Welker had been hit in the chest by a laser staff held by one of the giant creatures called the Babcottiatta. Welker's death led to his entire consciousness, memories, experiences, education, dreams, knowledge and all that he was to be transferred from a microchip that was in his brain to be uploaded to the intricate satellite system that had been developed by the Sikorsky scientists. As his brain patterns were transferred into computer script and sent from satellite to satellite and across several solar systems, one of one hundred clones of his body waited to receive the information on a secret location on Sikorsky's Planet. Welker woke up in a new eighteen year old body that was an exact replica of how he looked at that age. Many of his relatives had asked him about the experience of dying and then rising from the dead in a new, younger body. Welker told them all that he did not recommend the experience as he could still recall the pain of his death and the intense memory of being shuttled through several satellite transmissions to download into the new body. Welker had never married but had fathered many children with slave women at his property on Sikorsky's Planet. He allowed his children to be raised by other family members as he continued to study the mysteries of the universe. He had little patience for parenthood.

The MI chief of the *Wisconsin*, Major Alana Docker, was not related to the Royal Family. She was a brunette, about six feet tall with brown eyes and thin frame. She had a large scar on the left side of her face that she received in a fight against a wanted criminal back when she was a Lieutenant on Mars. The criminal was wanted for multiple murders and Docker had tracked him to one of the seediest housing projects on Mars. He had slashed her face during the struggle. She gave him worse and sent him to the morgue. The scar went from the end of her chin to just near her left eye. Docker had been a highly decorated officer and was married to her career. She had a daughter out of wedlock and allowed her to be raised by a maternal aunt on New South Africa. Last Docker heard, her daughter had become a tour guide on some decommissioned Battle Cruiser. Docker was silent as she watched the events on the view screens. She checked her utility belt that was over her shoulder and around her waist to ensure that she had her pouch of thermite grenades, her three laser pistols and compliment of stun darts and knives.

Docker looked to her right at some of the other junior officers in attendance and she wondered if they had the mettle to fight against the agile Kotek opponents or the brave men and women like DuBravac and Gillis. She smiled at one observation she made as she looked at the two Lieutenants to her right. They were both Spetsnaz graduates. That fact alone gave Docker some hope that they could repel the advances of Gillis and his group of rebels.

Spetsnaz graduate and Marine Corps First Lieutenant Lorenzo Winters was twenty-five years old and a man of few words. He had piercing blue eyes that seemed to pierce through any person. He had an ability to be able to determine quickly if he was being lied to or misled. Winters stood at six feet five inches tall, had dark hair and a lean, muscular frame. Winters had been assigned to the *Wisconsin* as a precaution against the risk of any unknown alien attack while in deep space. Admiral Gannon had wanted the best on his flagship and he requested Winters to be on the crew for that reason. Winters had been born and raised on planet New Berlin and had a large sibling group. His father was an elected representative on the UN General Assembly of that planet and his mother was a doctor. His father had several other wives and had twenty-seven children. Due to the father and the majority of the mothers having busy careers, Winters had been raised by servants. As soon as he turned eighteen, Winters left his family behind to attend the military Academy on Sikorsky's Planet. He married Admiral Gannon's granddaughter and was a member of the Royal Family due to that relationship.

Spetsnaz graduate and Weapons Tactician First Lieutenant Curtis Holton was a tall and muscular black man with light blue eyes and handsome face. He had been brought onto the *Wisconsin* by Gannon for similar reasons that Docker and Winters had been. Holton had been born on the planet Athena and left his family and friends to study advanced weaponry at the Academy on Sikorsky's Planet. He had several sisters on Athena and would make time to communicate with them at least once per week. His parents had been in the Criminal Investigation Division at the capital city of Athena and they died while attempting to apprehend the doctors that had created the Harcourt's. Holton had never married as he was not interested in having a family to tie him down and keep him from traveling. He had run the weapons section on the *Wisconsin* with an iron hand and left little to chance. He was friends with Lieutenant Zerbe due to the spare time they spent together on the long voyage to the outer realms and was disappointed that the Frenchman had become a traitor.

Holton wore his dark purple weapons section uniform with the logo of the *Wisconsin* on his shoulders and a web belt with weapons that rivaled those that Major Docker had on her. Holton was silent as he watched the view screens and listened intently to what the Admiral and Captain Rendon said. Holton would give his input when asked and not before.

Standing in the back of the command station area in her red uniform was *Wisconsin* engineering Lieutenant Commander Jason Smart. His long brown hair was held off his narrow shoulders by three hair ties. He had three collegiate degrees from Sikorsky's Academy, all in engineering, and regularly wrote research papers on new theories and technology. Smart was just under five feet tall and a bit overweight. He made no comments as the events unfolded on the several screens before them. He was not a member of the Royal Family and had little interest in politics or who won what election. As long as he could tinker with engines and publish his research he was content. He had been married for several years to his sweetheart from college and had two children that were in grade school on Sikorsky's Planet. Smart had resisted Gannon's request that he join the crew of the *Wisconsin* but he was not an Admiral that would take no for an answer. In return for serving under Gannon, Smart's children were given spaces in the most prestigious private school on Sikorsky's Planet. Although Smart hated being away from his family, he was willing to make that sacrifice for the best interests of his children.

Space Station Cy-5 Correctional Officer First Lieutenant Mindy Wei escorted two of her prisoners to the Command Station. Wei wore a black uniform as the officers for the correctional division were under the MI Branch. She was armed with a laser pistol and had a laser rifle strapped over her left shoulder. She was just under six feet tall and had short dark hair. She was originally born on a transport space ship that was traveling to planet New Sao Paolo. She spent most of her youth on that planet before she left to study at the Military Academy on London of Old Earth. While attending that campus, she honed in her skills to learn multiple foreign languages and earn marksmanship awards in her weapons classes. She was selected to serve in the MI branch due to her proven proficiency in languages and weapons. She stood by the two prisoners that she had brought up from the Tank so that her Captain could use them for whatever purpose he saw fit.

Space Station Command Sergeant Major Jan Granstrom had put in thirty-three years of service since enlisting at the age of eighteen. She was ready to retire and move back to her home world of New South Africa. She had received many awards, medals and promotions for her many achievements and acts of bravery from battles on planets New Berlin, New Vladivostok and New Edinburgh to serving as the top non-commissioned officer on board the Battle Cruiser *Amistad*. She was tired of the wars and the fighting. When she requested that her Captain transfer her to a less stressful environment to finish out her service, she was sent to Cy-5. She was aware that the man that had graciously granted her request for transfer, Bruce Allen, had died along with the rest of the Second Fleet. She mourned him and the other crew members that had given her so many years of good memories. Although she was now ready to retire, the officers of Cy-5 had ordered that she remain as their top enlisted soldier until order was restored to the eight solar systems. The current events meant that her freedom to seek a new life would be delayed.

The first of the two prisoners that Wei had brought from the Tank was Selena Ortiz. She was the sister of bar owner Joe Ortiz. She had been arrested during a battle on the second level of the space station which left twelve MI soldiers dead and an officer that was a member of the Royal Family. Selena Ortiz was thirty-three years old, well educated in finance and business and helped manage the bars belonging to her family. She operated as the accountant for the family and traveled extensively to many worlds. She had seen her share of violations of the rights of humans and aliens alike and accordingly had no love for the Royal Family. Her long dark hair could not conceal the bruises on her face from the beatings she had received from Wei and her prison guards. Ortiz had her hands cuffed in front of her by plastic twist ties and her legs were similarly bound to prevent any attempt at escape.

Lana Bauslaugh was the sister of Midnight. She had arrived on the space station with her full human husband and their seven children so that they could rendezvous with the rest of the family and enjoy some quality time together. The numerous insurrections put an end to those plans.

Lana had been drawn into the fighting and was captured. Her husband had been killed and her seven children were incarcerated in the infamous Tank. Lana had black and white fur and green eyes. The security professionals in the Tank had determined that due to her double jointed bone structure they needed to take extra precautions with her. Accordingly the placed a chain around her upper arms and torso, another short chain to cuffs around her ankles and cuffs around her wrists. She had whip marks on her back that were still healing from the torture she endured in the Tank. Wie herself had conducted the torture in an attempt to find from Lana the number of her family on the station and who was collaborating with them. Lana had not broken under the cracking whips that sliced her skin open. If she had any useful information, Lana refused to reveal it to Wie.

Astro-physicist Professor Caria Reed paced back and forth in front of the screens as she looked over the officers and the others as the rebels took the most important areas of the station. She had been assigned to the station as the chief of sciences. While everyone else was fixated on what to do about the rebels led by Gillis and Zerbe, she was more drawn to the massive explosion in the center of the solar system. When the eleven Red Javelin weapons erupted, all power on Sikorsky's Planet seemingly was disrupted. Reed wanted to know why and for how long. She was tuning out the military talk as she began speculating in her mind what form of energy was emitted from those weapons that would cause such a planet wide outage. Reed had her doctorate from the University of Monterrey on old Earth and like Jason Smart, she had been published numerous times.

Reed looked over toward the back entrances of the Command Station and counted fifteen MI soldiers and eleven Marines. All of the soldiers were combat ready with laser rifles in their hands and web belts stuffed with grenades, laser pistols, knives, stun darts and other weapons. Reed mused to herself that she was under dressed in that other than the two prisoners, she was the only person without weapons on her. She listened as the military schemed and pontificated.

"Why haven't they cut off our oxygen supply yet?" Gannon demanded.

"Because we have something that they want. They know that if they kill us that they will lose loved ones in the process. They know that we have prisoners here with us." Wei pointed to Ortiz and Bauslaugh. "They would kill their own if they did."

Sikorsky sat in his Captain's chair and nodded. Wie had a knack for cutting the discussion right to the heart of the matter. He believed that she would make a great Captain one day. "Correct. What we have now is a stalemate. They control the most important stations and we can kill people they care for. I want to speak to their leaders to negotiate with them."

"Our family does not negotiate!" Welker smashed his fist on a computer panel. "We are the Royal Family! We have sent several alien races to extinction! We have conquered eight solar systems! Those Kotek rebels should be on their knees before us, begging for their lives! We should send in our remaining MI and Marines and retake the engine room!"

"And then what?" Rendon pointed her index finger at Welker. "We can't leave because they have the docking area.   And even if we did what about any more attacks from the traitors on Robert Andrews? All of our Allen Fighter ships have been dispatched from the Wisconsin and most have perished. We probably have only a handful of pilots left to get us out of here safely. We don't even know if our family still has control of Sikorsky's Planet. We have ten planets and one moon in full rebellion and can do nothing about it because we just got out smarted by a bunch of civilians, some cat people and a platoon full of Marines that violated their oath! We should demand safe passage to the Wisconsin and leave this place."

"And go where?" Gannon paced as he considered their options. None of them were safe in his view. Whatever action they determined to take, there would be substantial risk involved.

"To one of the planets under our control," Rendon responded. "New Edinburgh is under our family control. There are other places. We would be safe there."

"In the meantime, those rebels out there have us under their thumb." Docker spoke up.

"I could take my platoon to the engine room and retake it," Winters offered.

"Do it and kill everyone," Sikorsky ordered. "We have to have the life support systems under our control. We will feign a negotiation while you get into position."

"Yes sir," Winters nodded.

"Sergeant Major, go with him." Sikorsky told Granstrom.

"Yes, Captain." she responded and followed Winters to the emergency exit.

"I should go as well," Smart spoke up.

Sikorsky nodded, "Go, Jason. They will need your

expertise in case they left any kind of explosives or traps."

It was assumed that the traitors would have locked down all of the elevators and sliding doors. To avoid detection they would have to maneuver using ladders and secret passageways to gain entrance to the engine room.

Sikorsky looked to Gannon and Rendon. "Which of us should perform the negotiations with the traitors?"

"It's your space station. You talk to them." Gannon waived his hand at him.

Sikorsky smiled and walked over to where the hostages were standing. He looked both of them in the eyes and ran his index finger under Selena's chin. She glared back at him.

"Touch me and I will bite your hand off." Lana promised him.

Sikorsky winked at her. "Watch your mouth. You are on thin ice, cat lady."

She hissed at him and bared her sharp fangs.

Sikorsky turned away from her and looked to the transparent metal observation window that was about eighty feet above him. He looked at the stars and considered the words that he would speak. "Computer, open a communication with the engine room, the weapons section and the docking area."

Gillis arrived at the engine room with his wife, Lila, Venus and Choi when the computer alerted them that the captain of the station wished to begin a dialogue with them. They entered the engine room and saw that Joe Ortiz and several of his daughters and some of the children of Midnight were working on the engine computers. One of them, a skinny Kotek with grey and black stripes over a patch of white fur and big eyes named Phoenix was hanging by his tail from the ceiling with a computer pad in his hands. He was coordinating some computer program with Krista, Nina and Melody Ortiz who were on the second balcony typing on holographic keyboards to his instructions. The squad of Marines that were loaned to them by Zerbe were on guard with laser rifles ready.

Joe Ortiz smiled and gave Gillis a bear hug as they waited to hear from Captain Sikorsky. They did not wait long. As Gillis was introducing his wife and friends to Ortiz they heard the deep baritone voice of Captain Sikorsky.

"Attention Les Gillis and friends. My name is Antonin Sikorsky and I command this station. I congratulate you and your friends on a hard fought victory. We should discuss a reasonable and mutually beneficial truce."

Gillis and Ortiz looked at each other for a moment. Both men were motioning to each other to begin a dialogue with Sikorsky.

DuBravac nudged her husband. "Say something."

Gillis cleared his throat, "We are always willing to negotiate, Captain. I believe that both sides will be better off if we can avoid any further bloodshed. Plus, I understand that the hull has already been breached in several locations. It is in your best interests to cooperate with us. I am listening."

Lila nodded at the group as she ran inside the engine room and began climbing up the ladders to the third balcony. She passed the Ortiz girls on the second balcony on the way up. Lila had been coached by Gillis to immediately begin to re-program the life support controls to her own hand held computer so that she could operate the oxygen controls from a distance. She began typing on the holographic computer pad on the third level as she began the long task. She tuned out the conversation between Phoenix and the Ortiz girls as she concentrated on the pass codes that Sapai Hu had given them from the docking area. Most computers in the engine rooms would shut down if a wrong password was typed in. She did not want to make such an error.

"Good, my friend. Good." Sikorsky said. "We should meet for drinks and discuss the terms. My command staff wishes to bargain with you for safe passage to the Wisconsin."

"And in return, what do we receive?" Gillis asked.

Venus was soon next to Lila and was helping her by placing magnetized scanners onto the computer desks. She smiled at Lila as she slid down on her back and crawled under her feet placing the scanners.

DuBravac walked inside the life support section that was connected to the engine room. She found that there were eight oxygen regeneration machines. She began placing magnetized explosives on each one and she synchronized the radio receiver detonator to her hand held computer. After she completed the task she sat down on the last swivel chair at the end of the chamber. She looked over the computer keypad in front of her and began typing in the security codes that they had received from Hu. She smiled when she gained security access and began downloading all controls to the oxygen regeneration machine number eight. She hoped that her husband would do a good job of stalling Captain Sikorsky. She was going to need more time to finish splicing the controls to her personal communication device.

"My friend, you and your loyal fighters will receive a complete farewell to hostilities by me and my soldiers and, in addition, we will hand over all prisoners that are related to anyone that is on your side." Sikorsky told Gillis.

In the weapons area, Zerbe listened to the conversation between Sikorsky and Gillis as it was being broadcast throughout the space station. Kim Ortiz and some of the Kotek weapons experts were scanning the inventory lists and keeping watch for any rogue space ships that might endanger the station. Giola and Porter arrived with Midnight as Zerbe turned to face them. Zerbe smiled when he noticed the Andolini girl. She was quite possibly the most beautiful woman he had ever seen. She smiled back at him and her mind recalled that she had seen him before, at the wedding celebration for Dia Cho and Felicia Essex. It had been over four years ago. He was the man that started the riot, the uninvited man that crashed the wedding. Giola moved closer to Midnight and Porter as they walked into the weapons area.

"Gillis and Lancer sent us," Midnight informed Zerbe. "They want us to synchronize all controls for the weapons area to our personal computers."

Zerbe nodded. He had grown more and more impressed with Gillis. "That is a damn good idea."

"We want all of the prisoners released, Captain." Gillis stated firmly. "You do that, we allow you to leave and take possession of the Wisconsin. I think we both know that the home planet of our little empire has lost the ability to communicate with either one of us. We are all in the dark. As far as we know the First Fleet and Sikorsky's Planet have been vaporized by that huge explosion. Our working together could spark a new beginning for humanity. We could be an example to the other planets by showing their populations that cooperation is the only way for humanity to survive this tragedy. I would welcome the opportunity to work with you sir and show the people that we can all work together."

Sikorsky smiled as he believed Gillis was being taken in by his ruse. "I agree my young friend. We should be working together. I have two hostages with me right now. Their names are Lana Bauslaugh and Selena Ortiz. I am willing to release them both and all of the prisoners in the Tank so that those individuals can assist us in achieving the common good for us all. Perhaps we should all plan on leaving on the Wisconsin together and travel to a neutral planet so we can each wait out the hostilities. Like you said, there may not be anything left to fight for. There are no longer sides to take in the conflict. The only motivation

I have now is survival for me, my crew and you and your friends."

"I am amenable to that arrangement," Gillis said to extend the conversation. "I have read up on you, Admiral Gannon, Captain Rendon and your XO Commander Welker and found that you are all brilliant tacticians. That is my major study at the Academy. I would like to have the honor and opportunity to meet all four of you and learn from you."

"And we would love to learn from you," Sikorsky said. "The tricks you pulled off on that Blood Moon were absolutely genius. If we all join forces we could be formidable."

"Then let's meet," Gillis suggested. "Just you and me. We can iron out our agreement and present the terms to our people. Where would be a neutral and acceptable location to you?"

Sikorsky thought it over. He had not yet received any notification that Winters and Granstrom were in position to attack. "The main cafeteria on the shopping mall level. We can meet at the open food court where there will be hundreds of witnesses around. We won't be able to surprise each other there and the noise level is not too bad so we can enjoy some coffee and talk."

"But it is wide open, Captain." Gillis said. "If either of us wanted to send in a sniper to take the other out it would be too easy. Also, one of the wheels was breached by that explosion. I am not confident that we would be safe there. I suggest another location for us to meet."

"Name it."

As the give and take was going on, Winters and his platoon of Marines and an additional platoon of MI soldiers slid down the ladders toward the engine room. Granstrom was with them and she had her laser rifle slung over her shoulder. They were able to hear the whole conversation as they methodically moved into position around the engine room.

Winters landed on the bottom floor level from the ladder. The doors to his right and saw a secret entrance onto the third balcony of the engine room. He gave his troops a closed fist which meant for them to stand ready around him.   They would wait for Sikorsky to give the word to attack. Winters had on his burgundy colored beret that signified he was in Spetsnaz. He had always enjoyed the respect and admiration from the soldiers that he received just because he had completed that Special Forces program. He saw the respect in their eyes as they waited for his next command.   Winters knew that taking the engine room would be simple. He had a well-trained platoon of Marines and several MI soldiers on his side. The enemy on the other side of the engine room were amateurs, circus performers and students.   Wiping them all out and taking the engine room back would be like taking candy from a child.

Winters kneeled down near the emergency entrance and was soon joined by Granstrom.

"What if this is a mistake," Granstrom whispered to him. "What if we can all walk away from this peacefully as that Gillis kid is suggesting?"

Winters glared at her, "We have our orders."

Smart moved in next to them. "Since I am the ranking officer here, let me lay the ground work. No shooting unless necessary. We take these people prisoner if we can. They are already upset. No sense doing anything to make them hate us more than they already do."

Winters snarled at that suggestion, "Look you may outrank me but this is a military exercise. You are only here to ensure that we can avoid any booby traps that those upstarts might plant while they have the station. My team and I are going to take that engine room and it will not be a pretty sight. So, Lieutenant Commander, if a little violence offends your sensibilities then I suggest you wait here while we do our job."

"I am ordering you not to fire on them unless absolutely necessary," Smart warned.

Winters pulled out his laser pistol and aimed it at Smart. "You don't have the guts to give orders. Get out of my way. Sergeant Major, enter the codes to open the secret doors."

"Yes sir," Granstrom said softly.

Gillis had suggested that Sikorsky meet him at Dos Gueros Muertos, which was met with a negative response. Sikorsky countered with the observation deck area where there would be no room for a sniper to hide.

"I accept," Gillis smiled. "I suggest you bring an escort and I do the same. We can make this a peaceful transition."

"Good. I will be at the observation deck in fifteen minutes," Sikorsky concluded.

"I look forward to meeting you, sir." Gillis said and then turned to see that his people were in position throughout the engine room. He walked inside and then turned to the right to see how his wife was coming along with the life support controls.

"Is the mutual love fest between you and Sikorsky over? I was getting jealous listening to you kiss his ass.

Mine is the only one that you should be kissing. Besides, his is probably hairy anyway." DuBravac kissed him playfully on the cheek.

"And yours is as smooth as baby skin. Any news for me?"

"All of the explosives are in place, my love." DuBravac whispered into his ear as she kissed him again. "And I put the charges on each oxygen regeneration machine to make sure that they cannot attempt to override my new passwords."

"I love you," Gillis kissed her on the cheek and then stepped out into the large engine area. He looked up at the top two balconies where the others were working.

"Almost done up here," the grey, white and black striped Kotek named Phoenix said from his perch on the ceiling.

On the second level balcony, Krista Ortiz was on her back and placing an occasional magnetic explosive on the base of the computer sections. Lila had taken care to instruct her on the proper placement and activation of the small three inch long and one inch wide device. Krista placed the explosive and allowed the magnet to attach to the metal frame before turning the top counter-clock wise two clicks which activated it for long distant detonation.

Lila had programmed each of the explosives to the frequency in her hand held computer. Once finished, Krista wriggled out from under the long computer table that extended out in a U shape and was about fifty feet long. She had placed ten explosives and it took her all of ten minutes to finish the task.

Venus kept moving on her back as she placed scanners all around the bottom base of the computers of the third level. Once she completed that task, she followed the instructions of Lila and began placing an occasional small magnetic explosive under the computer tables. If they were taken by the enemy soldiers, all they had to do was detonate them from another location and the Royal Family would have a useless space station.

"Lila, I'm almost done," she reported.

Lila had her communication device in her right hand and was typing something on the small keyboard with her left. Within a few minutes, she had finished the directions that Gillis had given her. He wanted them to be able to leave the engine room and the life support controls but still maintain dominion over them from a distance. She now had that control downloaded into her personal hand held holo-com. "Okay, everything is relayed through my holo-com. We can control all of the engineering controls from a distance as far as fifty kilometers away."

Venus moved into a sitting position. Her red sweater had been pulled up as she had been crawling on the metal floor and exposed her midriff. Three of the men on the third level were checking her out. Being a super model, Venus was accustomed to being stared at, especially when she was in some of her photo shoots wearing very little clothing. She smiled at the men gawking at her and pulled her sweater down over her toned stomach. "Then let's move. We're needed at the Tank."

Lila was about to stand up when three metal wall panels on the third level slid open. She attempted to cry out when she saw several Marines and MI soldiers charge through the openings with laser rifles ready. One of the soldiers pointed the end of his barrel into her face. Lila froze in place looked over her left shoulder with her eyes only, afraid to even turn her head, and saw that Phoenix had flung himself onto the rails below. His big eyes showed fear in them. He made eye contact with her. Lila had her right hand hanging over the side of the metal rail. She dropped her holographic communication device over the rails and down toward Phoenix. She prayed that Phoenix would be able to catch the device without attracting attention from the soldiers that were filing onto the balcony. The soldiers surrounded the three men, Venus and Lila.

Phoenix flipped himself down to the floor on the lower level and ran toward Gillis. "Sir, soldiers! They somehow came in through the third level."

"Damn," Gillis drew his laser pistol and noticed that Midnight was by his side. He had instinctively not trusted Sikorsky. The fact that the soldiers had arrived confirmed that Gillis had been correct in his lack of faith in the man. "Pass the word to the others. We are being ambushed."

Phoenix handed Gillis the gadget that Lila had dropped down to him. "She made certain that I had this."

Gillis nodded and placed her communication tool in his pocket. He did not want to consider blowing the hidden explosives as long as Lila and Venus were on the upper level and in harm's way. He would have to come up with a different plan so that he could get the two girls and the three men to safety.

Winters walked out onto the third level and had his laser pistol in his right hand. He looked over the five prisoners before him as his soldiers were aiming downward at the traitors below. He was a bit surprised at how easy it had been to take the cadets and the rebels. The blue prints of the space station designs were fairly common material that was studied in the engineering classes at the Academy. He wondered if the cadets had overlooked the potential danger from the hidden security passages.

"No one move," Jason Smart yelled down at Gillis and his team. "We have you out numbered and out gunned. You fought well, but now it is over."

DuBravac pensively waited behind the protective walls separating the engine room from the life support station. She pulled out her hand laser with her right hand and her holo-com device with her left. Her device was vibrating which meant she had received a document from source. She pressed the red button on the upper left of her communication device and a ten by ten inch three dimensional color screen appeared about three feet from her face which revealed that Lila had sent her an encrypted document. She opened it and found that her dear friend had given her the frequency codes necessary to detonate the explosives on the third floor. She smiled and slowly took a look out the door and saw that her husband, Midnight, Phoenix and all of the others were hopelessly surrounded. She quickly moved back behind the wall to avoid detection.

Winters was confident that he had complete control over the situation. He smiled as he looked over Venus. He enjoyed her choice of clothing, her black shorts and a tight red sweater that accentuated her curves. "You. Aren't you one of those bikini models?"

Venus nodded slowly. She was shaking from the fear of the moment. Winters walked up to her and was inches from her face. "You are even prettier in person. I think I am going to interrogate you personally."

"Leave her alone," Lila said boldly and moved toward them.

Lila felt overly protective of the Andolini girls. The entire Andolini clan had been kind and inviting to each of the Gorski Gang members. Lila and Jurgen had been treated as if they were members of the family ever since the Blood Moon Incident. The tension in the engine room was beginning to reach a boiling point.

Winters glared at Lila and laughed, "You going to do something about it?"

"She's my friend. Leave her alone. We surrendered. You got the engine room back. You don't need to be bothering her any further."

Winters backhanded Lila, causing her to stagger backwards and hit the metal wall. She held herself up with her left hand and covered her face with her right. Her cheek was stinging with pain.

"You are a fucking asshole!" Venus barked at

Winters as she tried to move toward Lila to help her.

Winters grabbed Venus' left arm and held her in place. "You aren't going anywhere except with me to become my personal play thing."

"Okay!" Gillis yelled up at the large group of soldiers. From his observation point on the floor level, he could see that things were rapidly getting out of hand. "You win. We give up. We are all going to lay down our weapons. Just leave the two girls alone! Sikorsky, if you are still listening, and I know that you are, call off your dogs."

Granstrom moved next to Winters and had a look of anger on her face. She had expected better from a Spetsnaz officer. "Lieutenant, they are surrendering. Don't make this any more complicated than it needs to be."

Winters stared at Granstrom with a look of defiance in his eyes. He pulled Venus up against him and wrapped his right arm around her waist. He enjoyed how her body felt against his. Venus thought of trying to struggle but Winters put the barrel of a laser pistol to her head. Winters moved his hand upwards and cupped her left breast in his hand. "Don't move poster girl. You are coming with me. Sergeant Major, kill everyone else."

Jason Smart was on the other side of the third

balcony checking some of the solar power cell levels on the large U shaped computers when he heard the command. He turned his head in the direction of Winters and pointed his left index finger in his direction. "I told you I am in command here! I am ordering all of you soldiers to stand down! There will be no shooting of civilians and anyone that has surrendered will be treated with dignity and respect!   Those are my orders!"

Winters sighed and aimed his laser pistol in Smart's direction. He had been wanting to eliminate the engineer for some time. He was nothing but an egghead and Winters had little use for him. As he pulled the trigger, Venus reached back with her right hand and dug her finger nails into Winter's face. He screamed in anger as she wriggled free from his grasp. His shot narrowly missed Smart and harmlessly fizzled out on the metal wall near the engineer.

Winters tried to grab for Venus as she ran for the stairs but she was already out of his reach. He then attempted to aim his laser pistol at her but was tackled from behind by Lila. She had rushed at him and dived with her hands outstretched into his exposed backside and sent him falling forward from the force of her shove. Winters landed on the metal floor face first and lost his grip on his laser pistol and his prized burgundy beret fell from his head onto the metal floor. Lila grabbed the man by his hair and began smashing his face onto the metal floor as Venus ran for the stairs to get away.

Granstrom and another Marine pulled Lila off of Winters. Lila was kicking and screaming for the soldiers to let her go. Winters stood up to his feet with rage on his face. His nose was broken and he had blood on his upper lip and chin. He was breathing heavily and his lips were curled back as he started toward Lila with his balled fist raised in the air.

"Everyone calm down!" Smart ordered.

"You bitch!" Winters snarled at Lila as he pulled out his twelve inch blade knife from its sheath on his web belt. "I am going to cut you open!"

Granstrom moved in between Winters and Lila. "She is my prisoner, Lieutenant. I am responsible for her safety. You are out of line, sir. Put the knife away, step back and let us finish this mission. Now sir."

Winters glared at the woman and looked over his shoulder at two MI sergeants. "Arrest Sergeant Major Granstrom for disobeying a ranking officer."

The two sergeants looked at each other with a confused stare, seemed unsure of what to do.

As the drama was unfolding, Krista Ortiz led her

two sisters down the stairs from the second balcony to the engine room floor. The three women stood against the wall and looked upward at the stand-off between Winters and Granstrom. Venus was at the ladder for the third floor and watching with concern, her heart pounding in her chest from the stress of the events. She had a clearing where she could escape but did not want to leave without Lila.

DuBravac had sent as an encrypted message to the communication devices of Jurgen and Harcourt that contained the programs that Lila had forwarded to her. Of all the individuals that had arrived with her on the *Blue's City*, they were the two she trusted most. She then ordered her own communication device to engage a one way conference with multiple parties so that they would be able to hear what was happening in the engine room. She connected with Lancer, Zerbe, Harcourt, Rolf and Doernitz. After she had finished with each of those moves, she kept her laser pistol in hand so that she could cover her husband and friends if they needed to make a quick escape out the front entrance.

"Lieutenant, your sergeant major is correct," Gillis bellowed. "We have surrendered. The engine room is yours. There is no need for violence. We will go with you peacefully to the Tank. All I ask is that you give me a face to face meeting with the commander of the station. As a Spetsnaz officer, you were trained in the code of honor for the military. You know that you must treat us in accordance with the laws of the Code of Justice. Any combatants that have duly surrendered must be afforded safe and humane housing. I demand that you provide that for me and my friends."

While Gillis was speaking, Midnight made head gestures toward some of his family members to follow him upwards. Gillis said nothing as the Bauslaugh's were slowly inching toward the pipes where they could easily climb to the computer stations above where they would be able to leap upward. Confrontation would be bloody, but Midnight had a keen eye for putting his people in the best position to fight back.

Winters laughed hysterically and pointed his knife down at Gillis. "The Code of Justice? There might not be any government left and therefore no courts to enforce the laws! We are now dealing with the laws of Darwin. Survival of the fittest. So, this is how it is going to be. I want the super model given over to me or I start firing. It is that simple. Once she is in my hands then we will take the rest of you to the Tank and that will be the end of it."

Gillis was cognizant that Venus was on the ladder

that was between the second and third balconies. She shook her head at Gillis as if to tell him that the request made by Winters was okay with her. Lila had risked her own safety to help her to escape. Because of that, Venus would not leave her behind. She started climbing upward, seemingly to offer herself in sacrifice so that her friends would not be fired upon. As she ascended the ladder steps, Midnight slowly moved toward the ladder from the floor level to the second level. None of the soldier seemed to care and the middle balcony concealed Midnight from their view. He began to climb up the metal ladder with a stealth that impressed Gillis. The other Kotek' were getting ready for what they believed to be a confrontation. Their tails were wagging nearby the ledges and pipes they were near. Gillis had seen them move when Nappy, Midnight and Mittens helped him in the docking area. These soldiers had probably never been exposed to that level of speed by an opponent before.

"I am all yours," Venus announced to Winters as she made it to the top of the ladder. "Now, can you stop this and let my friends go?"

Winters smiled as he looked over the beautiful woman before him. His eyes studied her lovely face and full breasts. She would make a stunning trophy wife for him. If she refused to submit to him he would just take her by force. Winters had concluded that the government was gone due to the explosion created by the eleven Red Javelin weapons. The eight solar systems would naturally slip into anarchy and nihilists would rise to be led by despots and tyrants. It would soon be a world of every man for himself. The meek would not inherit the galaxy and a lovely lady would make the inevitable life of danger and dubious future easier to take.

"Take the rest of them prisoner and escort them to the Tank." Winters ordered as he grabbed hold of her arm.

Granstrom and Smart breathed a sigh of relief. They were both concerned by the unstable actions of the Lieutenant. A squad of Marines began to descend the ladder to take the rest of the traitors to the Tank. Midnight was waiting on the second level with a few of the other civilians that had been with them at Dos Gueros Muertos. They remained still as the soldiers climbed down past them and to the floor level. Midnight calculated how many more were on the top level. He was elated to see that they were splitting up their forces. That would not bode well for them in combat.

Unknown to all of the occupants of the engine room, Francois Zerbe had heard the events over his holo-com, thanks to DuBravac's quick thinking. Zerbe led C.J., Summer, Snowflake, Bear, Luna, Patch and seven of his Marines to the outside entrance to the engine room. They were all armed with laser pistols, knives, grenades and ready to fight.

Summer took in a deep breath through her nose and leaned into Zerbe. The fur on her back was raised upward and her tail was fluffed up. "There is stress, fear, anger and many other smells from the feelings inside there. We might cause more harm than good if we rush in."

Zerbe nodded. He had learned to respect the instincts of the cat people. "Okay, we wait out here. Hopefully they will come out this direction and we can ambush them and rescue our people."

Gillis did not struggle as a Marine began to frisk him. Gillis remained silent as the soldier removed his two knives, stun darts, the communication mechanism that belonged to Lila and his own. The soldier tossed the weapons aside but handed the devices back to Gillis, concluding that the tools would be harmless. Gillis thanked the soldier and immediately placed the devices in his side pants pocket located on his left leg. Gillis observed in silence as the rest of the team were having their weapons removed. He hoped that none of the soldiers thought to go inspect the life support control room as they would find his wife hiding there. Soon all of the team with Gillis were unarmed.

"Now that I have control over the engine room, my soldiers will escort you to the Tank." Winters voice was loud and echoed off the high metal ceiling of the engine room. "Any attempt to escape and my Marines will cut you down. Sergeant Major, lead them to the Tank and have them processed. Commander Smart and I will keep the MI soldiers here with us so we can start gassing the rest of the civilians. With any luck we will have this station back in working order very soon."

"Move out, Marines!" Granstrom yelled as she grabbed Lila by the arm to lead her downstairs. The Marines began pushing the several Kotek's, civilians and Gillis out through the door.

Winters watched as the soldiers escorted the prisoners out of the engine room and toward the outside hallway. He held Venus close to him, savoring the thought of her as his prize possession. He used his free hand to feel her breasts and felt the lust growing in his loins for her. He smiled at her and she glared back at him and was silent as she stood with the arms of the cruel man around her. She did nothing to stop Winters from feeling her body in the hopes that his fondling her would cause him to be too distracted when the right moment presented itself.

Venus observed the engineer Smart typing on the computer pad at the end of the third balcony. His brow furrowed with confusion and he raised his head and looked directly at her. She was accustomed to having men undress her with their eyes. But this stare was something different.

"What did you and your friends do to the security codes?" Smart asked.

Venus swallowed, "I have no clue what you are referring to."

Smart looked down at the floor level as the prisoners were almost all outside. "Then perhaps one of them know. Winters, stop them. They changed the security protocols. Whoever did this is a damn genius."

"I thought they were just a batch of hot heads with weapons," Winters mumbled. He raised his voice to give his next order. "Sergeant Major! Stop and bring the prisoners back inside."

There was no verbal response to his order.

Out in the hallway, Zerbe and his small squad had taken the first squad of Marines without a sound. Gillis, Lila and the other prisoners had disarmed their captors when Zerbe surrounded them. Granstrom has been the first to surrender her weapon. She had her fill of the fighting and fundamentally disagreed with the manner that Winters had handled the situation. She had no desire to be part of another massacre; her only thought was to find a way to safely leave the space station.

Unfortunately many of the Marines did not wish to surrender. The other three squads began to fire their laser rifles; most of their shots missed their targets. Some of the shots that were on target actually hit and killed their own Marines. The screams of the individuals hit by friendly fire could be heard back inside the engine room. Winters, Smart and the MI soldiers gave each other alarmed looks. Venus merely smiled as she realized that her captors were about to get a taste of justice.

Zerbe fired into the cluster of Marines with C.J. by his side, firing a laser pistol in her right hand. She was quite accurate in her aim, killing three female Marines on her own.

Phoenix slashed a female Marine across her throat with his claws and kicked a second over the balcony. Gillis joined the conflict, firing his laser pistol at the Marines and killed two men quickly. The laser fight was over in under ten seconds.

The members of the three squads of Marines that

had fought were all dead. Their bodies were either ripped open by laser fire or their throats or abdominal areas were gashed by the claws of the Cat People. Lila turned her head from the sight due to the large amount of blood and internal organs on the metal walkway. The stench of the burnt flesh of the laser wounds was putrid and Lila covered her nose.

"Look, we didn't want to be involved in any of this," Granstrom whispered to Gillis. "Winters is not well and the station captain is only concerned with self-preservation. I just want to lead what is left of my unit to a ship to get safe passage to the Wisconsin. We can help each other out if that is truly your goal."

"Well, then, you won't mind going back in there and asking Winters in a nice manner to let my friend go?" Gillis suggested.

At that point they heard Winters shouting his commands to return to the engine room.

"They still have about fifteen MI soldiers inside," Summer warned Gillis.

"Leave them to me," Granstrom suggested. "I know you have no reason to trust me or the rest of the platoon, but I assure you that we can handle the situation."

"But Venus is still inside," Lila hissed with anger.

"I will get her out for you," Granstrom promised

them. "I will need a few of you to start trickling in behind me with some Marines. Make it look good to Winters that we are complying with his orders. I will tell him we were ambushed but we caught a few of you and killed the rest."

"Lead on," Zerbe responded and pointed to Bear, C.J., Phoenix, Summer and a few Marines to follow the Sergeant Major into the engine room. Gillis walked with Granstrom into the large chamber and noted that the MI soldiers were leaning over the balcony and aiming their laser rifles downward. Venus was still being held by Winters with a laser pistol to her head. Smart ignored the situation and continued typing on several holographic keypads in an effort to break the new security codes entered by Lila. His frustration was evident on his scowl and the beads of sweat on his upper lip.

"Lieutenant, we were ambushed," Granstrom said truthfully before she lied to him. "We repelled the attack and these are the only rebels left alive. They killed a lot of our Marines, but the situation is under control."

"Good," Winters dismissed in his mind the loss of life. All he cared about was getting the control of the engine room back to Smart. "Now, I need to have the new codes so the engineers can take control of the station. Speak up. Don't be shy. I will give you ten seconds to give them to me or I start killing people. Or, better yet, I start shooting furry people. You cat-humans make me sick."

Bear hissed after hearing Winters racist remark. He wanted to rip his throat out.

From her hiding place in the life support section of the engine room, DuBravac activated her holo-com and patched herself into the explosives that Venus and Lila had placed along the engine room. If the MI soldiers started shooting she would start blowing up the upper level so that those on the floor level would have a chance to escape. At least the magnetic explosives would eliminate the snipers and give Les and the others a chance to flee in the chaos that would inevitably follow.

But she never had the chance to detonate the explosives. From deep space a squadron of small Allen Type fighter space craft approached the space station from the west. Amy and Joe Ortiz saw them coming from their laser canon positions in the weapons room. The ships were from Robert Andrews moon and they were on a clear attack pattern.

"Can we call them off?" Kim Ortiz asked into her tear drop microphone that was wired into her hand held communication appliance.

She looked over in the direction of Snowflake who

was placing a teardrop microphone over his head and attempting to contact the pilots that were rapidly closing in on the space station. Snowflake attempted several languages to explain that the Sikorsky's were no longer in charge of the station. Wolvie was also trying to raise them on the main communication system. His arm was still bandaged from his wound, but he seemed to be working well.

"They are not responding!" Wolvie yelled to the others in the weapons section.

"I have tapped into their communications," Snowflake reported. "They have orders to destroy this station! There is endless chatter about some virus that was unleashed on their moon and that they want revenge against the Royals for that. I am relaying to them that there are several hundred innocents on board but they are not breaking off the attack!"

In the Command Station, Captain Antonin Sikorsky made his own attempts to contact the pilots in the squadron. He was met by the same frustration as Wolvie and Snowflake from the weapons area. Sikorsky looked over to Admiral Gannon, Captain Rendon and Commander Welker with fear in his eyes.

"I recommend we abandon the station," Sikorsky

said softly.

"All of the remaining Allen Fighters and Rausmschiffs from the Wisconsin are in route to engage the rebels. But the previous skirmishes have diminished our forces significantly. We do need to get off this station and do as Gillis suggested. We need to get back to the Wisconsin where we would have a fighting chance."

"Agreed," Gannon stood up from the comfort of the sofa he had been relating in. "Lieutenant Wei, bring the two hostages with us. We will need them to barter for safe passage out of the docking area."

"Yes Admiral." Wei pointed a laser pistol at Lana Bauslaugh and Selena Ortiz and motioned toward the exit with the barrel. "Move it."

"Perhaps I should get down to the weapons section and offer my assistance," Lieutenant Holton suggested. Since the Ortiz and Bauslaugh families were in possession of the defense systems, and none of them were trained tactical officers, Holton concluded that an experienced hand would be a welcome addition. "I can hold off the attackers to some extent while you negotiate with the rebels in the docking area."

"Do it," Rendon barked as she ran toward the exits. She hoped that the engineers and computer technicians had been able to replace the majority of the damaged parts of the *Wisconsin*. "And hurry."

Holton motioned toward several female technical sergeants that were standing against the wall to follow him. They did not comment as they moved for the exits. The amateurs that took over the weapons area would be no match to defend the station against aggressive and experienced fighter pilots.

The engine room heard the entire discussion from the command area. Winters was vexed as he would be forced to deal with the traitors led by the Ortiz family. In doing so, he would lose his prized poster girl and quite possibly would be treated harshly for his actions.

"Lieutenant, you have no choice now." Gillis yelled up at him. "We have to work together or this station is going to be peppered into Swiss cheese."

Winters looked into the eyes of Venus in the hope that she found him attractive enough to forgive his brash behavior and could see only anger there. He slowly released her arm. "Go to your friends."

Venus slowly walked away from Winters and toward the ladder leading downward. She slid down the sides as she could not get away from the man fast enough. She was met by Lila who hugged her close.

"I should take these MI soldiers to the weapons area," Winters suggested. "We all have some experience in tactics. In the meantime I suggest that the rest of you free the prisoners in the Tank and get everyone to the Raumschiffs in the docking area. If those rebels hit the nuclear-solar converter cells, this station will explode in a chain reaction in seconds."

Lila nodded to Gillis, "He's correct about that. We really should escape this station. Now, Les. Now."

Zerbe stepped forward as he sensed that majority of the Bauslaugh and Ortiz faction were too terrified to act. "Les, you, me Granstrom, Bear, CJ, Summer, Phoenix, the few Marines we have left and Lila should head to the Tank. Everyone else needs to move it to the docking area. If one of those ships makes a direct hit on the coils, we are all dead. Move out!"

Everyone began to move in different directions as they could hear the loud shrill of the warning klaxons that signaled that an attack was imminent. Gillis ran to the wall where his wife was hiding and found her crouched down with her communication apparatus in her hand. Their eyes met and he grabbed her left hand.

"Honey, let's go." Gillis said over the sound of the alarms. "Time to abandon the station."

Sophia nodded and stood up. She ran out of the life support area and the engine room, hand in hand with her husband. She placed her mechanism in her pants pocket as she ran and drew a laser pistol, just in case. Her heart pounded in her chest due to the adrenaline and the stress. She knew full well that the alarms meant that the space station was about to perish, either by explosions or hull splits or both.

They followed Zerbe, Lila, Granstrom, seven enlisted women, Bear, CJ, Summer, Phoenix and a few of the Christians from the Ortiz faction down the east hallway. They were running as fast as they could, their boots and shoes clanging on the transparent metal walkways.

Gillis handed Lila her communication device back which she used to immediately contacted her husband, warning him that the ships in the docking area needed to be up and running as they all needed to make a quick escape.

Joe and Amy Ortiz were surprised when the weapons section Lieutenant named Holton arrived at their location. He had his hands in the air as did his crew of weapons technicians.

"We are unarmed!" Holton yelled to them. "We are here to help out. What is the distance of the squadron in relation to this station?"

Joe Ortiz smiled and leaned over the rails. "Fifteen kilometers and closing fast!"

Holton led his few technicians up to the second level of the weapons area and directed them to take over some of the empty laser canons. He sent three others to start loading armor piercing missiles into the rocket launchers.

"What can I do?" Snowflake asked Holton with a sound of relief in his voice.

Holton smiled at the solid white Kotek and nodded to the solid black one behind him. "They will need help loading the missiles. Thank you."

Snowflake and Wolvie ran on all fours toward the technicians that were loading missiles onto large eight wheeled racks to make it easier to push them toward the rocket launch silos. One of the technicians reached down and scratched Wolvie on the head as she had never seen a Kotek that looked so cute before. Wolvie, enjoying the attention of the female technician, rubbed his face on her leg and made a noise to her that sounded like a "Ma." He really liked it when she started scratching him behind the ears.

Holton sat down into a laser canon next to Amy Ortiz. His adrenaline level was at an all-time high. He counted twenty fighter ships on his computer generated three dimensional targeting grid. He was angry that the pilots on those ships would not respond to their attempts at communication. Because of their unwillingness to respond a lot of innocent people were about to die. He took about five seconds to note that there were several space station small fighter ships engaging the rebel ships out in the distance. There were also some small Allen Type fighter ships that had the colors of the Wisconsin that were in the middle of the battle. All of the ships were firing at each other. Holton saw three small ships erupt in explosions of flesh and metal as he quickly adjusted the seat in his lease canon. As Holton assessed the situation he wondered just how much the rebellious civilians on board the space station had to do with it. He glared at Amy. "You know how to do this?"

She smiled at him and saw that his expression was stern. She correctly concluded that he believed that she and her family had somehow invited the attack, which was not what had happened. The ships from the moon had no connection to the Ortiz family at all. She decided it would be best not to engage in a debate over the history of the events. "Yes sir. I can handle myself."

Holton pulled the headphone set over his ears and

used his hands to begin pinpointing the approaching ships. He locked onto the Allen Type fighter that was closing in on his left side. He did not hesitate and fired the laser canon as he was aware the damage that one of them could cause to the space station if they were able to penetrate the defenses. He felt the laser canon device rock backwards from the force of the energy release. He saw on his targeting grid that he had scored a direct hit. The ship exploded in a brilliant flash of white, orange, yellow and light red. He did not pause to celebrate as there were many more ships that needed to be destroyed.

The other technicians and cat people were firing their weapons as well as the three of the rebel space craft's began firing armor piercing rockets at the space station. The missiles began hitting areas where tourists would have been staying at hotels or in the shopping mall areas. The missiles slammed through the metal hull and exploded in the interior of the station. People were screaming in panic as many were lucky enough to die in the explosions and the less fortunate were swept out into space. Just under three hundred people died due to the hull breaches.

One missile impacted the hull just under the weapons section and exploded. Joe Ortiz, who was operating one of the laser canons, was caught in the blast.

He screamed as shrapnel ripped into his torso and rear. Three of his followers and two of Holton's technicians were also hit. They were killed instantly as most of their bodies were obliterated in the hail of flying shrapnel and fire. The hole in the hull was causing the oxygen to be sucked out of the weapons area.   One of the technical sergeants that was loading missiles into the silos lost her footing due to the power of the suction and was pulled into the hole in the hull. The hole was a mere one foot in radius and her legs were sucked in but she was trapped at her buttocks. She screamed in agony as her legs were dangling out in space and her torso and head were inside the space station.

Winters and his MI soldiers arrived at that moment and immediately began to take over the laser canons that had either dead or wounded seated on them. Winters pulled Joe Ortiz from his laser canon seat and laid him on the metal floor. He surveyed the numerous wounds in his body and immediately knew that the situation was hopeless.

"I'm dying," Ortiz stated the obvious. His body was riddled with metal, his mouth and chin covered in blood that he was coughing from his lungs.

"Hang on, old man." Winters took his outstretched hand.

"My daughter is on the laser canon over there, next to the officer." Ortiz said with his voice growing weaker with each word. His head was motioning toward Holton and Amy Ortiz. "Please get her, get her off this station. Gillis was right. I should have listened to him. We should have left."

Winters looked over at Amy Ortiz and liked what he saw. She was petite, had an attractive face, nice curves. He smiled to himself. He lost the model girl but this one was a good replacement, he thought to himself. "Do not worry about your daughter. I will keep a very close eye on her."

"Thank you," Joe Ortiz gasped one last breath and his head sagged to the side.

Winters closed his eye lids with his right hand and stood up. He saw that everyone was fighting bravely but no matter the level of commitment, the situation was futile. He took his place in the laser canon that had been occupied by Joe Ortiz and began to look for something to shoot at.

Zerbe led his small team down the stairs to the bottom of the station and toward the Tank. He found that the metal doors were wide open as the jail guards had fled in a panic. Gillis motioned to Lila and Sophia in the direction of the large office where the controls were located to open all of the cells. The two women immediately rushed to the office entrance and found to their disappointment that the metal doors were locked shut. Seeing that the metal entrance was not accessible, Bear, Summer, Phoenix and CJ began using their claws to rip through the walls that were made of simple sheet rock. They had a hole dug out for Lila and Sophia in seconds. The two women rushed inside and found the controls and began typing on the keyboards to release all of the prisoners.

As they did so they could feel the station shaking from the impact of laser fire and explosions.

Typing furiously Lila looked up at the others. "I have the doors opening! Get ready for an exodus of prisoners!"

"All of the other security measures are down!" Gillis followed. "They should have no impediments to making it up here to the entrance!"

Down in the Tank, several hundred men, women, children, Akarzdamedians and a few Koteks watched as their cell doors swung open. They went from outright panic due to the rocking of the space station from the outer space attacks to elation in that someone had freed them. They began to run up the hallway to freedom and hopefully to find a safe way off the space station. Mothers and fathers were carrying their children as they ran.

Gillis and Zerbe were waiting as the crowds began to come into their line of sight. Zerbe threw two glowing twists down the hall just in case the power on the station went out.   Gillis and CJ were beckoning the crowd as another rocket hit the station. The people were screaming in fear.

"Come on!" Zerbe yelled over the klaxons and the screams. "Come on! We need to get off this station!"

Several of the prisoners would express gratitude and bless them. Others were silent as they passed by Gillis and Zerbe. Summer, Phoenix, CJ and Bear helped with some of the children. Fortunately the younglings seemed to like the half cat half human Kotek's and went to them willingly.

Midnight and Panther arrived with numerous members of the Ortiz family at the docking area. He observed doctors and nurses helping people on board the numerous Raumschiffs and transport space craft. Midnight was met by Lancer, Giola and Harriak. All four fell to the floor as another explosion occurred and twisted the space station violently. There were screams among the nurses and civilians. Sergeant Kolb and her remaining squad did their part, helping to calm the crowds.

"What is wrong with those assholes?" Harriak demanded. "Don't they know that there are civilians on this station?"

"Clearly they do not care!" Midnight yelled over the sirens and the screams of the people. "Gillis and Zerbe are bringing several hundred prisoners just behind me. The weapons section is not faring well at all."

"I'll go," Giola quickly volunteered.

"No, I will." Harriak put his hand on her shoulder. "You are young and need to escape this death trap. I am old and have lived my life. I was trained on laser canons years' back when we used them to blast holes into the grounds to speed up the mining process. I can do it."

Lancer knew that the man was volunteering to sacrifice himself. He shook Harriak's hand, "Godspeed my friend."

Harriak left them behind as he sprinted down the corridor to what was certain to be the end of his days.

Midnight turned to see that Mittens and Odyssey were now standing at his side. "You two get a line started so that we can have an orderly boarding of the prisoners onto the space craft. We don't want people trampling on each other in a panic."

"What can I do?" Giola wanted to help out.

"Stay by my side," Midnight told her. "Keep your com device ready as I am certain we will be getting a call from Gillis or Zerbe soon."

Another explosion rocked the station and everyone in the docking area fell to the west side of the room as the station began to lose gravitational controls.

Sapai Hu screamed from the balcony where the control tower was located. "The hull is splitting! The computer reports that the hull to the ring of the station is splitting open! We have to leave now!"

People were rushing to board a ship, any ship, to avoid dying when the ring of the station cracked and swept them all out into space.

Admiral Gannon, Captain Sikorsky, Captain Rendon, Commander Welker, Lieutenant Wie, a few soldiers and their two prisoners arrived to see the scene of many trying to board a few ships. In the distance, Sikorsky recognized the Super Raumschiff that belonged to Rendon and Gannon. They all noticed that several civilians were trying to board their ship as the rear access ramp was extended and resting on the floor of the space station.

"They are taking my ship," Gannon growled.

Welker laughed and aimed his laser rifle at a family of five that were running toward the ship that Gannon was complaining about. They were mere peasants and had no right to be taking their space craft. The ship was reserved for an Admiral and members of the Royal Family and it was time to enforce the rules and bring some form of order to the chaotic situation. The caste system of Royal Family members on top and the rest beneath them needed to be enforced. Welker was ready to pull the trigger when Rendon stopped him.

Rendon put her hand on Welker's arm. "Are you nuts? There are about a hundred people here. They will turn on us without a second thought. Put the weapon away."

Welker glared at Rendon and the peasants in the docking area. He wanted to start firing as the lower class were nothing but target practice in his mind. Most of them were lazy beggars that humanity would be better off without. He decided to follow Rendon's orders, just in the slim chance that she might have a good reason for sparing the people that took up space and used valuable oxygen that should be given only to those worthy. "All right, I will play nice for now. But these sheep have taken too many liberties and they need to learn their place."

"And they will," Rendon snarled at him. "But now is not the time."

Midnight noticed from a distance that his aunt Lana

was being led in with chains on her legs and wrists. She must have smelled his scent as she looked directly at him and smiled. Selena Ortiz was next to Lana chained in a similar manner. Midnight growled in a way that made his aunt Panther, Lancer and Giola take notice. It was a guttural growl that Midnight had only made when his family was threatened. Giola had her laser pistol ready as she concluded the growl was menacing in tone alerting them to potential danger. Lancer watched as Panther and Midnight both dropped down on all fours and their fur on their backs and their necks rose up. Without warning, they both charged in at full speed in the direction of the four highly ranked Royal Family members in the distance.

Lancer immediately realized what was going on when he saw the black female Kotek in chains with the Royals. He aimed his laser rifle in the direction of the four Royal Family members and noticed out of the corner of his eye that Giola was in a kneeling position pointing her laser pistol in the same direction.

Lieutenant Wie saw the two solid black cat-human hybrids charging them before the others did. She kicked Selena Ortiz to the floor and drew her laser pistol to defend herself. Welker saw the action as well and his eyes went wide when he saw the two large cats charging them. He began to pull his laser rifle around to fire on them. Rendon ordered the other soldiers with them to kill the two charging Kotek animals. The soldiers began to comply and started to aim their laser rifles at them.

Napoleon, also known as Nappy, saw the commotion near the south side of the docking area. He was directing civilians onto a ship that he was going to pilot. He stopped what he was doing and began running toward the four Royal family members in an effort to support his family members.   The calico colored Kotek was not as fast as his other family members but he still ran about triple the speed of an average man. He closed the distance on the group that were holding Lana hostage.

Before Welker or Wie could open fire, Lancer and Giola fired first. Wie did not see her death shot coming. The burst from Giola's laser pistol split Wie's skull open sending blood and brains onto the wall behind her. Her body twisted backwards and slid to the floor and slammed into the wall behind her.

Welker was hit by Lancer's laser rifle burst. Rendon screamed as she watched Welker's chest explode open. His corpse flipped backwards, head over heels, and landed on the metal floor with a thud.

The soldiers with them seemed stunned that the two

officers just died in front of them. Most of them were looking around them with confusion in their eyes, trying to determine who had fired on them. One of the soldiers spotted Lancer and Giola in the distance. He aimed his laser rifle in their direction and was about to fire when Lana slashed his arms with her claws. He screamed and dropped his laser rifle to the floor. She leaped onto his back and then bit into his throat with her powerful jaws, sinking her sharp fangs into his flesh. Selena Ortiz began crawling to safety as she had no weapons to fight back with, but the cuffs on her hands and ankles made the act difficult. By now several civilians were screaming and running out of the line of fire.

Rendon, Sikorsky and Gannon had now drawn their laser pistols and were ready to fight back. Gannon aimed at the female Kotek named Lana and fired at her twice. Lana's chest was sliced open by the laser beam. She let out a horrible scream of a wounded animal and released the soldier she was attacking. She flew to the ground and slid on the metal floor on her side. She was panting and crying in pain. The soldiers were also firing wildly at the charging creatures, some of them cursing as they did so.

Laser fire was flying wildly throughout the docking area. Some civilian non-combatants were hit inadvertently and fell dead. Others were being trampled by the hysterical civilians that were running here and there in sheer panic.

Nappy leaped into the air and tackled Sikorsky to the metal floor and began to rip the man to pieces. Sikorsky screamed in fear at first and then in agony as he felt the sharp claws shred through his flesh. He tried to hit Nappy with his closed fists as the Kotek sank his fangs into his throat. Sikorsky bled out on the floor. All the while, due to the murder of Lana, Nappy was growling in a manner similar to the way Midnight had.

Rendon fired her laser at Midnight and her first shot ripped into his long tail, severing it from his body, leaving only a few inches of tail remaining. Midnight screamed in pain as the second laser shot from Rendon sliced his upper right shoulder. Midnight fell to the ground and slid several feet. Panther was unscathed and leaped onto Rendon with her claws extended. Rendon let out a shrill scream as Panther's claws tore her stomach open. Rendon's stomach, intestines and other internal organs spilled out onto the metal floor. Panther released the woman and allowed her to fall to her knees and then slump face first to the blood stained metal floor.

The other soldiers under the command of Gannon were still firing when the entrance of the docking area was soon full of people rushing in. It was the hundreds of prisoner's from the Tank and they were running like there was no tomorrow to board one of the many ships that awaited them. Everyone had heard the warnings from the computers that the station had a growing split in the hull of the wheel of the space station. Sophia and Gillis were the first two inside and saw the melee before them. Without hesitation, they both began firing in the direction of the enemy soldiers. Lila joined them in the fire fight, carefully aiming her laser pistol and firing at the men and women in the black uniforms. The soldiers suffered loss of limbs and were dropping dead due to their accurate aim.

Gannon tried to make his way toward his Super Raumschiff that was being boarded by many civilians. Gannon began firing into the crowd, hitting several dozen people in the back with his laser pistol. Fathers, mothers and children were falling with gaping wounds in their chests as Gannon stepped over and on their corpses on the way to his ship. His reign of death came to an end when the Kotek named Stripes leaped onto Gannon's back and tossed him against the wall which was fifteen feet away. Gannon slammed into the wall, had his breath knocked out of him from the impact and dropped his laser pistol. As he slid to the floor several of the civilians that lost loved ones or family members that he had been shooting at charged at him. Gannon screamed out loud that he was an Admiral and a member of the Royal family and that they should worship him. Those cries only encouraged more anger in the mob of people. They began to stab at him with knives, cutting him over one hundred times before Gannon's screams ended.   The Admiral died and there was not one soul left on the space station that cared to mourn him.

Engineer Smart determined it was time to leave the engine room. He directed the few remaining with him in that location to make haste to the docking area. He climbed down the ladder to make his leave of the engine section when another armor piercing missile hit the station. The explosion shook the entire station and caused Smart to lose his grip on the ladder and he fell about the equivalent of one floor to the metal floor of the engine room. Smart realized that everyone else was gone as he rolled over on his side and was fighting to catch his breath. He could hear the computer voice warning of the imminent destruction of the space station. Smart pushed himself up and grabbed his left side as he felt stinging pain. He was certain he had broken a rib or two in the fall. He began running as fast as he could with his labored breathing slowing his pace. He heard more explosions and could hear the sound of explosive decompression as oxygen was being drawn out of the station from the holes being blasted into her hull.

Winters finally left his post on the laser canon and ran to the side of Amy Ortiz. He heard the loud noise of the hull beginning to split open. He screamed at her to follow him as the time had come to abandon the station. Amy screamed back at him that she needed to find her father. Winters, realizing there was no time to argue with the woman, grabbed her into his arms and threw her over his shoulder. As he carried her kicking and screaming he saw that Holton, Snowflake, Wolvie and Choi were screaming at the others to run. The writing was on the wall, anyone left behind was a dead man or woman walking. Amy was livid at Winters for treating her in such a manner as he refused to let her go.

A nurse named Cobb helped a doctor named Felton carry the injured Midnight toward one of the transport ships.   Selena Ortiz followed as she felt indebted to the solid black Kotek. Lana's corpse was left behind, lying on the floor near the remains of Rendon, Wei, Sikorsky and Welker. Doctor Felton had been able to stop the bleeding on the shoulder and tail of Midnight and had administered several injections to help ease his pain. Midnight was soon unconscious from the medicine given to him and his head hung downward until his mother, CJ, approached and took his head in her hands and held it level to his body.

In the control room Sapai Hu turned to her friend Dainia Mills who was screaming at her over the sounds of the explosions, the klaxons and the grind of rending metal. "Sapai! We need to leave now! Look at the computer screen!"

Hu looked over the shoulder of her friend and saw that the upper section of the center piece of the space station, where the Command Station was located, was blown apart by three of the small fighters. The station rocked back and forth and Hu was shaking with fear. She left her home in Cambodia to see outer space. Never had she dreamed that she would be in the middle of a life and death struggle in the middle of deep space. There would be no rescue teams to save them. Their only hope of survival was to follow them man that had been brandishing the bloody sword earlier.

"Dainia, let's go now! Hurry!" Hu screamed.

Mills looked at the younger girl with a look of sadness. They had grown into close friends during their short time together on the station. Mills realized that the hull was about to rip apart under the stress of the tears and the rotational movement. She concluded that only one of them could leave. The other had to stay behind and operate the controls so that the civilians and the space craft could safely depart. "You go! I have to stay to seal off the emergency bulkheads so that all of the space craft can successfully leave the station. Go, Sapai. Go."

Hu was silent as she realized that her friend was going to stay behind and die. She hugged Mills close to her and when she heard another explosion she ran for the exit and toward the numerous space ships below. Mills turned her attention back to her computer screens and began typing commands to begin the process of sealing the secondary bulkheads so that she could depressurize the docking area so that all of the ships could make a safe exit. Mills hoped that Hu would have a long life, find love and have many healthy children. Mills had known love twice in her life, once with a pilot that came into her life and left as quickly as he had arrived. It was a stormy love affair that Mills recalled with a smile on her face. Her second love had been Hu. She never told Hu how much she loved her as it potentially would have harmed their friendship. Mills never had feelings for another woman before, but she had them for Hu.

Hu reluctantly joined the others on the lower level. She saw the man that had the sword strapped to his back and ran toward him. "Sir! We have to go now! The station is going to split into several pieces very soon!"

Gillis looked at Hu and nodded. She could see the stress on his face as he was directing people onto the space craft. His wife was standing by his side and helping him encourage the mass of people to hurry on board the space craft. He pointed toward the Blue's City. "Sapai, get on that ship over there! That will be one of the lead ships when we depart and we will need your knowledge of computers to help save all of these people!"

Hu nodded. "Yes sir!"

Sophia watched as Hu ran off as her husband had ordered. She saw in the distance that Bear and Lila were directing the stragglers from the engine room and the weapons section toward the ships that still had some room. Winters, Holton, Amy Ortiz, Choi, Smart, Wolvie and Snowflake were running to board the ships.

"We almost have everyone on the ships!" DuBravac yelled.

"Get on the Blue's City!" Gillis told her. "We need to leave right away."

Sophia grabbed his hand and kissed his lips softly and ran off. She watched her husband waving his left arm at Bear and Zapata to hurry and join them. Lila smiled at

Gillis as she helped a family of seven that were seemingly the last to arrive. Lila lifted two young children up in her arms and instructed the mother, father and the other children to quickly follow. Bear took a teenage girl in his muscular arms and was running for the Blue's City just behind her.

Another explosion shook the station from the engine room area. An armor piercing rocket scored a direct hit into the nuclear reactor which caused a chain reaction of explosions. W.C. Harriak had stayed behind in the weapons room to keep fighting the small space craft. He was firing rockets from the silos and had destroyed two more of the enemy ships. He felt the station shaking and was terrified of the tearing sound of metal. He knew the end was coming. He kept firing at the ships in the hope that he could take as many of them with him so that the others would have a better chance of escaping. He had grown to like the cadets on the *Blue's City* during the short time he had spent with them and wished them well. He had lived a long life and wanted the same for each of them.

Dainia Mills realized that they had only a few minutes before the reactor would reach a critical level and explode. When that happened, everyone would be dead. She looked down and saw that there were only a few people left that were boarding the ships. "Hurry up," she whispered to herself.

Doernitz had strapped himself into the pilots seat of the Super Raumschiff called *Admiral One* that had belonged to the Wisconsin officers. He had the ship powered up and all of the security checks were done. His co-pilot was a young woman named Ortiz; she was smiling at him as she watched how easily he guided his fingers over the controls and had the ship ready in no time. The ship had the capacity of carrying up to sixty people comfortably. Doernitz was well aware that the ship had about three times that number of people on her. He hoped his wife Lila was one of them. During all of the chaos neither one of them had the time to call the other on their communication tools. Doernitz knew that escaping the station was one obstacle to survival. The other would be fighting off the remaining small fighter ships that were still out there.

Rolf Rhinehard leaped into the pilot seat of a large transport ship and had completed all of the safety checks necessary to depart. The seven Bolt widows were on board and in one of the lower levels of the space craft. They all seemed to cling to Rolf and he found that he actually enjoyed the attention of the seven lovely women. He recalled that DuBravac had given him the advice to take on several wives and was starting to think that was a really good idea. Sitting next to Rolf in the co-pilot seat was a bloodstained calico colored Kotek that had introduced himself as Nappy. It was the closest Rolf had ever found himself to a Kotek. He couldn't help but think how cute the half-man and half-cat looked.

Lancer was seated next to Harcourt in the pilots section of the *Blue's City*. Their ship was ready for lift off and he waited for Gillis to give him the order. Standing behind the two pilots with a pensive look on his face was Zerbe. He had no patience for being surrounded by the scared civilians below. Zerbe felt he would be better served in the upper section with the two pilots as the mass exodus occurred. Zerbe's skill set on the tactical board would be needed to fight off the Allen Fighters that they would soon face.

Karla Ortiz, Mittens, Lucius and Porter were the designated pilots for other transport ships. All of those ships were crowded with scared civilians that let out cries each time an explosion occurred. The pilots of each space craft instructed the ship computers to seal the entrance ramps so that they could lift off, save the *Blue's City*.

Gillis jumped with both feet onto the loading ramp leading up to the rear of the *Blue's City*. He could hear her engine running and saw the faces of men, women and children huddled in the loading area of the space craft. DuBravac smiled when she saw that her husband was on the craft with her.

"Just one family left!" he called out to her. "Once they are on board we are getting off this station!"

She smiled at him. Standing next to her was the Kotek named Phoenix. His grey, black and white striped tail was wagging in the air as he was happy to see Gillis safe.

Lila led Bear and the parents of the last group of children toward the *Blue's City*. They heard a loud explosion behind them and felt the temperature rise rapidly in the docking area to their rear. Lila was about five feet from the *Blue's City* and looked over her shoulder to see why there was so much heat rising. What she saw made her blood run cold. There was a gaping hole in the hallway at the northern entrance to the docking bay. The opening was about ten feet wide and six feet tall. The cuts on the metal were jagged as if the hull had been ripped open by some form of explosive device. She could see the darkness of space through the hole. Realizing that they had little time before the oxygen would begin to be swept out into space, she screamed and began to run faster. Her heart was pounding in her chest as she forced herself forward.

The husband and wife running behind Lila were screaming as they lost their footing due to the suction created by the hull breach. Their screams were not heard over the roar of the removal of the oxygen into outer space. The husband bounced on the metal floor as he tried to grab the slick metal floor of the docking area. His efforts were futile as the partial vacuum created by the rapid loss of air was too powerful. His last hope was that his five children would, by some miracle, live through the horrific event. His wife was soon sucked out through the hull breach and joined her husband in death. Their oldest daughter also perished as she slid on the metal floor and her prayers to her deity went unanswered.

Bear was able to leap onto the loading ramp to the *Blue's City* and he successfully held on to the two infants in his arms. Several of the others in the lower level of the ship reached with outstretched hands and grabbed onto Bear and others relieved him of the burden of the two terrified children.

Lila felt the suction of the vacuum pulling on her as she struggled to step onto the loading ramp of the *Blue's City*. She had twin three year olds in her arms which limited her ability to grab hold of the walkway rails and left her at the mercy of the elements. Keeping her balance was proving to be impossible and she realized that she was fighting a losing battle. She would soon join the other three that had been swept out into the blackness of space.

In an effort to save their friend, Gillis had quickly ordered several of those watching to assemble a train as he grabbed the belt of DuBravac and she in turn grabbed hold of the back of Giola's pants. The three boldly ventured out onto the ramp in an effort to save Lila and the twin girls. Gillis felt that two of the Kotek's, Phoenix and Stripes, had grabbed hold of him from the back and were anchoring the group by holding onto the metal mesh walls of the loading area. Giola walked rapidly onto the ramp and reached out with both hands and grabbed hold of Lila's left arm with her right arm.

Lila realized that her weight along with the force of the vacuum would be too much for Giola. She handed the child in her right arm to Giola and smiled as the younger girl took hold of her with her free right hand. Giola passed the child over her shoulder to DuBravac who repeated the act by giving the screaming girl to Gillis. That act freed up one arm for Lila and she was able to grab hold of the loading ramp rail on the right side of the ship. By now, her feet were off the ground and she could feel the force of the suction. She gritted her teeth and handed the second child to Giola.

Giola struggled to keep her grip on Lila as she quickly handed the second screaming child backwards to another group of the passengers that had created a second assembly line to help save the girl. Armed with the solace that both children had been saved, Giola began trying to pull Lila inside. Giola could feel the wind whipping behind her and her long, dark hair was flying all around her face. She saw the terror in the eyes of her friend and she tried to pull her toward her. Lila struggled to hold both Giola and the rail as she felt the girl slowly pulling her inside.

"Pull her in!" Gillis screamed as he held onto his wife's pants loop and leather belt. He was deeply grateful that the acrobatic Kotek's were holding him steady as the rapid loss of air was a force he had never experienced before. "Start walking backwards! One step at a time."

Each of the people began slowly pulling Lila inside. The young cadet let go of the rail and grabbed the thick red sweater of Giola with her right hand. She held on tight as her life depended on it. As they all walked backwards, Giola could feel the fabric of her sweater tearing from the pulling stress created by Lila's grip. She screamed out a warning that her sweater was tearing and grabbed Lila's right wrist with her free hand. She did so just in time as her sweater tore in half and was sent flying down the large docking area toward the open hole in the outer hull. Giola held Lila tight and screamed as she felt DuBravac pull her hard toward the inside of the space craft.

Lila fell into the *Blue's City* on top of Giola and the two women were face to face. Phoenix immediately pressed the button on the wall to seal the back entrance and retract the loading ramp. The back entrance slid shut in just three seconds and there were several of the over sixty witnesses in the lower chamber of the *Blue's City* applauding the heroic teamwork that saved the two young twins and Lila.

Lila held her right arm in pain and breathing heavily. Her heart was pounding in her chest due to the stress of the moment and the rush of adrenaline in her body. A nurse with a name tag that read "Cobb" rushed through the crowd to check on her. She concluded quickly that Lila had dislocated her shoulder.

"I broke two of my fingernails, too." Lila said to Cobb and looked up at her friends as DuBravac hugged her.

"Thank the Stars that you are safe," DuBravac told her.

"Thank you, all of you." Lila hugged her back and began to cry in her shoulder. She had almost died. She had never felt the sting of terror as she had in those moments when she felt the suction of the vacuum.

DuBravac could feel Zapata shivering as she wept, "It's okay, Lila. It's okay. You are safe now." she repeated several times in an attempt to sooth her friend.

Giola was brought in for a group hug as they felt the *Blue's City* moving forward out into space. Perhaps they would survive the day after all. Although Giola was topless, she seemed unconcerned that many of the males were eyeing her full breasts with great appreciation. She made no effort to cover herself, as her only thought was that Lila was alive.

"Those are the most amazing tits I have ever seen," a loading dock technician whispered to Stripes.

Stripes did not respond out of respect for Giola but silently agreed with the man. Gillis finally put a blanket over Giola's shoulders to cover her.

Giola pulled the blanket over her and held it tight as she realized that several of the men were still staring at her. She was suddenly embarrassed that she her body had been exposed to so many strangers in the packed loading area. Feeling as if she had to say something, she smiled at them, "Did you all like what you saw?"

One of the rescued prisoners, a young bearded man with dark hair that Giola estimated to be in his twenties, raised his hand. "I didn't get to see them."

His voice sounded as if he were very disappointed. Giola shrugged and opened the blanket and showed off her breasts to the man. He smiled, "Wow. Very nice."

Giola covered herself up, "Anyone else here that didn't get to see me naked?"

To her relief, no one answered. She surprised herself by the fact that she so willingly showed off her body the way she had. She walked over to the ramp leading to the upper levels of the space craft to get away from the crowd and to avoid some other person requesting to have her show off her body again.

CHAPTER TEN

In the upper level where the pilot section was located, Harcourt and Lancer were elated when their computer screens indicated that the back doors had sealed shut. They concluded that they were now ready to escape the crumbling station. Zerbe ordered them to make best speed toward the *Wisconsin*. Lancer was quiet as he silently mourned the loss of his closest friend, Hill. He followed Zerbe's direction and urged his space craft to increase speed. He instructed Zerbe to use the tactical computer array to detect any approaching enemy ships.

Dainia Mills had watched the rescue of Zapata and the children on the monitor screens in the control tower. Detecting no further individuals on the docking area floor, she sealed the secondary bulkheads and opened the outer walls. The numerous transport ships were soon exposed to outer space and could now flee the "death trap" of Space Station Cy-5. She sat back in her swivel chair and pulled out a pack of cigarettes from her breast pocket. Smoking had been outlawed on all space stations and military space craft centuries ago. Mills slowly pulled out one of the cigarettes and fumbled in her left leg pocket for a lighter. To hell with the laws, she thought to herself. She was going to die anyway. When she had been much younger, she had feared the idea of dying. She often questioned how a God or Gods could be so cruel to make her mortal. But now she had no fear. She had been able to decide how and when she would die. It was her decision to remain behind so that others could live.

"The Gods be damned," Mills muttered to herself as she sucked on the cigarette, feeling the warmth of the smoke in her lungs. "I got to follow the example of the Blood Moon Heroes by sacrificing myself for others. I know that Les Gillis and the other survivors will live to bring a new peace to the universe. It will be done by the hands of women and men, just like me. I am ready to face what comes next. When I get to the next life, if it even exists, I will spit in the face of the first deity I encounter."

Doernitz watched with a thin smile on his face as the outer hull began to slide open. He nodded to Krista Ortiz, his co-pilot on the *Admiral One* and she smiled back at him. Standing behind them were two other survivors of the space station battle, U.N.S.C. *Wisconsin* MI chief Major Alana Docker and Professor Caria Reed. When the carnage had begun, the two women were astute enough to flee the command station of Cy-5 and make their way to the docking area and locate the space craft of their now deceased Admiral Gannon.

They observed in silence as Doernitz skillfully guided the *Admiral One* out of the dock and out into the void. He had not yet been informed of the near death experience that his wife had gone through. Doernitz observed through the transparent metal that surrounded the front of the ship and he noted that there were still dozens of Allen Type fighter space craft circling one another and firing lasers and rockets. Bright laser bursts lit up the darkness of space, which caused many civilians that were watching out observation windows to gasp in horror.

"Some of them are from the Wisconsin?" Doernitz asked out loud to Docker.

"Good guess," she responded and pointed over his left shoulder. "The Wisconsin is over that direction. Get us close to her. With Gannon, Welker and Rendon dead, I am now her ranking officer. Patch me in to her command station. I will order them to lower their defenses long enough for us to negotiate entry onto her docking area."

"Yes ma'am," Krista responded and began to flip some of the switches on the control panel before her. "You are on."

"This is Major Docker. Admiral One is returning for docking and we need cover. We are bringing with us several other transport ships. The space station is about to self-destruct and we need to make best speed out of here."

They did not have to wait long for the response. "This is Technical Sergeant Jiao. We are ready to receive you. All of our officers are either in the small fighter ships that are engaging the rebels or were on the space station. The weapons section will give you cover if you approach from the north-east. That path is clear of the rebel fighter ships at this moment. Where are the Admiral and the Captain?"

Docker placed her hands on the back of Doernitz' chair as she saw the *Wisconsin* coming into view. "The Admiral, Captain and XO are all dead. Only five officers made it off the station to my knowledge and they are with us, Smart, Winters, Holton and Zerbe."

"What about Lieutenant Commander Krobben and Ensign Cheller?"

"Presumed dead," Docker answered coldly of her two fellow officers. They had lost any contact with the two officers soon after the fighting had started on the station. Docker assumed they had been killed and had not given them a second thought until Jiao mentioned their names.

"Most of our pilots are lost," Jiao informed Docker. "Those that are left are fighting the rebels. I am afraid we might not be going anywhere, ma'am."

"So there are no pilots in Level One to fly the ship?" Docker more demanded than asked.

"No, ma'am. They all took to the small fighter ships to engage the enemy."

"I saw you on the Blood Moon, Mr. Doernitz. You are a very talented pilot. Think you can fly a science cruiser?" Professor Reed spoke up.

Doernitz looked over his shoulder at the two women and realized that they did not know much about his background. He had learned that talent as a young teen-age boy from his adopted father Admiral Yamamoto. "Yes, ma'am. I have been the lead pilot on a Battle Cruiser before. Just tell me where we are going and I will get you there."

"Good," Reed looked a bit relieved as she shook her head at Docker. "Good."

Lieutenant Lorenzo Winters had made his way onto one of the several transports that were leaving the crumbling space station. He sat alone in a dark corner as other civilians and military personnel were cheering their departure. Winters had been briefly treated by a doctor named Jones and was informed that his nose was broken. Winters closed his eyes and was grinding his teeth together. The vision of the scratches on his face and his broken nose were all he could think of. The two that had damaged his once perfect face were going to pay. If it was the last thing he did, he was going to kill Venus Andolini and Lila Zapata. No one did to him what they had and lived to tell about it.

No one.

Rolf had taken the chief pilot seat of an eighty person transport ship next to an Akarzdamedian pilot named Szpuk Troven. Due to the lack of space on each of the ships, Rolf's transport space craft had over two hundred people cramped inside. They were all standing in cramped space, some crying and shaking with fear. Others, including Bolt's widows and Mayne, stood with a look of defiance in their eyes. The women had every faith in the abilities of Rolf Rhinehard to get them to a safer destination. The two pilots followed *Admiral One* out the rear of the crumbling space station and were the second ship to escape doom. As they entered deep space, Rolf ordered the computer scans to display a three dimensional view of the station behind them. He observed multiple explosions on the outer hull of Cy-5. He smiled when he noticed that the Blue's City was right behind them. He counted twelve other space craft that made it safely out of the docking area of the station. He stopped counting when a massive explosion sent metal shards out into space. The brilliance of yellow, white, red and orange splintered Cy-5 into millions of pieces.

"We barely made it," Troven observed in broken English with a thick Akarzdamedian accent.

Rolf nodded. He hoped that all of the ships were out of the docking bay before the destruction of the station. His first thought was to contact the other ships and determine how many made it to safety. Unfortunately the dozens of single seat fighter ships that had been intent on the demise of Cy-5 were turning their deadly intentions towards the escaping space craft. Rolf cursed under his breath and gripped the steering column that was a simple two foot long, one inch wide, black and red controller that was in between his legs. He jerked to the right to avoid a strafing run from a fast approaching small fighter that had red letters indicating it was from Robert Andrews Moon. The laser fire narrowly missed Rolf's ship.

"Look," Troven pointed with his brown, elongated

fingers. Rolf followed what the alien was directing his attention toward.

"Thank Baelder," Rolf whispered with relief as he watched seventeen one seat fighter ships from the *Wisconsin* engage the ships from Robert Andrews. White and yellow laser fire ripped through the darkness of space, lighting up the void. Rolf used the steering column to increase the speed of the transport ship and guided her toward the Wisconsin. The ships protecting them were outnumbered by the enemy, so it was only a matter of time before they would be targeted again. Their best chance for survival was to land in the docking bay of the Wisconsin and hope that the weapons section had enough laser canons and R-5 Rockets to repel any further aggression.

Lucius Andolini had a similar experience while flying another large transport ship. His co-pilot was a cat person named BB. They avoided a few laser bursts that had been fired in their direction and the ninety people in the belly of their temporary metal encased space craft cheered them on. For Lucius, it was a surreal feeling, knowing that the lives of so many rested on whether or not he could guide the space craft to safety.

BB placed a black, furry hand on his shoulder and smiled at him to give him a silent encouragement. "You are doing well, my friend. Keep your cool. You are doing well."

Only eighteen of the ships made it off the station safely. Several others were lost in the explosion that annihilated Cy-5. One of the eighteen transport ships exploded when hit in the rear by laser bursts from a Robert Andrews small fighter craft. Seventy-nine lives were lost in that explosion. Lucius and BB witnessed the destruction of the other space craft and shared similar thoughts: that they did not lose any one that they cared about in that explosion.

Doernitz flew the *Admiral One* directly at the rear of the Wisconsin. "Docking Bay in ten seconds! We are coming in hot!"

Docker and Reed held each other's hands as they watched their ship enter the rear docking area at rapid speed. Their fears of dying in space were replaced with the dread feeling that Doernitz would not be able to decelerate in time and that they would crash into the balconies of the docking bay. To their mutual surprise, Doernitz did something that they had never observed from a pilot. He slowed the space craft down by flying in circles in the large docking area. He made seven complete revolutions, avoiding any collisions with the balconies or the metal ceiling, before safely landing the space craft.

"I think he can fly the Wisconsin," Reed whispered to Docker.

Doernitz turned his swivel chair around and looked at Docker, "I'm going up to Level One with Karla and Krista and we will get the Wisconsin moving toward the Virginia. Send all the people we can muster to the Weapons Section to defend us. Who is your tactical commander?"

"Commander Krobben, but we think she's dead." Docker responded. "But you don't give orders on this ship, cadet. I am the ranking officer."

Doernitz stood up after releasing his safety harnesses. "You command nothing, ma'am. With all due respect, nobody that came from that space station will trust anyone with the Wisconsin logo on their uniform. That stunt your Admiral pulled in the engine room was unacceptable. If you attempt to exert control over this situation you will have a riot on your hands and you will lose."

"You going along with this rebellious talk?" Docker directed her question at Karla.

Karla smiled as she stood up, "Damn right. You people caused a lot of innocent deaths. I believe that the commander of this ship should be Les Gillis."

Docker snickered, "A cadet?"

Doernitz nodded, "Damn right. All of the people here will follow Les because he has demonstrated that he has every ones best interests at heart. I fought by his side on the Blood Moon. He is a natural leader. You want to survive this? Put Gillis in charge and let him guide us to a safe location. Deal?"

Docker nodded with reservations. She hoped that Gillis and the rebel would deal fairly with her. "Any further orders, Mr. Doernitz?"

"Yes, send my wife to the engineering room to inspect the repairs to the dark matter converters. I will not trust any of your officers' reports. She is the only person with the proper training that I would trust to clear us for full flight speed."

Doernitz and Karla did not wait for Docker to respond as they both slid down the ladder into the second level of the Raumschiff. They were met with thunderous applause from the crowded area. Doernitz directed all of the occupants to immediately exit the ship and to head to the weapons section to fight for their lives.

Rolf landed his transport next, followed by Lancer and Harcourt on the *Blue's City*. Gillis immediately opened the rear loading ramp and was the first to exit, followed closely by Sophia, Lila, Giola and Bear.

"Where to?" Sophia asked.

"To the weapons Section," Gillis responded. "Lila, get to the engine room and check on the repairs on the dark matter converters. We need to make light speed or better before more rebels attack."

"Yes sir," Lila smiled and hugged Sophia before running up the several flights of metal stairs.

Each of the remaining seventeen ships landed, one after another, into the safety of the docking area.

Porter was co-pilot on board a private vacation cruise ship that had fifty passengers who had been rescued from the Tank. The hull of the space craft was painted blue and green with observation windows all around. Porter smiled nervously at the woman next to him. She was in her forties with a long scar over her mechanical left eye which looked just like her normal right eye. She had light pink skin and a nice smile. She worked as an employee for the vacation company and had introduced herself as Zjaron (pronounced "Sharon"). She was born on Cootron and had served as a Space Command pilot for several years before entering the private tourism business.

"I think I crapped my pants," Porter told her.

Zjaron giggled as if she were a pre-teen in response to his comment.

CHAPTER ELEVEN

The Weapons Section was a mess when Gillis ran into the entrance. The racks of laser canon cylinders were not stationed near the rows of laser canons. The metal slides that should have been filled with R-5 Rockets were virtually empty. He noticed that Technical Sergeant Jiao and seven female technicians in red one piece uniforms and black boots were operating two laser canons in a feeble effort to defend the integrity of the space craft. Gillis could not blame the eight weapons technicians as they were operating a section that would normally require eighty to one hundred staff. Jiao smiled at Gillis and the new arrivals.

Gillis barked orders to Sophia, Giola, Choi and a few of the survivors from Dos Gueros Muertos Bar to occupy every third laser canon. He pointed to Bear, Nappy and Wolvie to help load R-5 rockets into the launchers.

Holton arrived a few minutes later and noticed that Gillis gave him a wary gaze. Holton cleared his throat, "I can help. I know how to operate these weapon systems."

Gillis pointed to one of the unoccupied laser

canons, "We could use more help there."

Holton nodded and walked rapidly to the laser canon. Although he had rank and status as a Spetsnaz graduate, he understood that the civilians had little to no faith in anyone in uniform. For the occupants of the Wisconsin to survive the day, they would all have to co-exist for their mutual benefit. The time to struggle for who would ultimately be in charge of the vessel was an issue to be determined at another time and place.

Sophia sat in the plush black and red leather seats of the nearest twelve feet high laser canon. As she secured her over the shoulders harness, the computer three dimensional display appeared before her which gave her a view of the carnage surrounding the Wisconsin. She closed her eyes for a few seconds, counting her blessings that they had made it off the space station in time. She opened her eyes to the tragic scene of chunks of grey, black and blue metal, all in different shapes and sizes that had jagged edges with scorch marks from the explosions. The computer display warned that there was a presence of magnetic radiation where the Cy-5 once was. Sophia heard the voice of Wolvie in her ear, informing her that her laser canon was armed with a fresh and fully charged canister. Sophia activated her targeting grid and took aim with her joystick and pressed the red button on the tip and fired a two foot radius red and yellow laser ball at a fast approaching Allen Fighter ship with markings indicating it was from the Robert Andrews Moon. Her aim was true and she smiled as the space ship erupted into an explosion of flesh and metal.

Sophia noticed that the Wisconsin was moving rapidly to the east. She concluded that Doernitz was in the pilot's seat on Level One and that he had control of the space craft.

The additional manpower turned the tide in the battle. The remaining opposing one seat fighter ships were dispatched one by one as the Wisconsin closed in on the Virginia.

Doernitz was a very skilled pilot. He was able to maneuver the ship so that the Weapons Section could exact pinpoint damage to their adversaries. Karla Ortiz was seated next to him in the Astral Navigation chair, charting the safest course to the *Virginia*. Krista Ortiz took a seat at one of the tactical stations and typed in orders for the computer to display the full view of space outside the Science Cruiser. Docker, Reed, Harcourt, Zerbe, Lancer, Mittens, Dracula, Stripes and Hu joined them, taking positions on the tri-level, rectangular Command Station. Hu took over the communications seat on the third balcony and begged for the fighters from the moon to cease their aggressive behavior. Lancer assumed the Captain's chair with Docker taking the Executive Officer position.

"Sapai, scan the Virginia for life signs and get us a read out on the condition of her ability to fly and support a crew," Lancer ordered. "Jack, contact the medical section for a report on the injured. Francois, see if you can get a team together to get us a head count on how many people are on this ship with us complete with identities and their training background. We are going to have to split the survivors between the two Cruisers."

Zerbe nodded and motioned for Mittens and Stripes to assist him in completing Lancer's directive. Harcourt contacted the medical section and Hu began working on determining the relevant information regarding the *Virginia.*

"Mister Lancer?" Hu spoke up after operating several of the long range scanners. "The Virginia has one life form on board. The computer indicates that it is a dog."

"A dog?" Docker raised her eyebrows.

"Yes, ma'am. A dog. Golden Retriever to be exact. The weapons section is fully functional and has no evidence of any usage. The engine room is fully functional, life support systems are able to sustain a full crew and the food and water reserves are at one hundred percent."

Lancer nodded, "Any computer memories or security tapes as to the fate of her crew and cargo?"

Hu shook her head, "I cannot access the security tapes. That would have to be done from the inside. I can, however, order that the docking bay open so that we can land as many ships on her as we wish."

Lancer smiled, "You just earned your pay for the day. Do it. We will send over a small group to investigate and take control of the ship. Les, any suggestions on that?"

Docker frowned as she had no clue that Lancer was conducting business over a live feed with the Weapons Section. She bit her tongue and said nothing to avoid confrontation. The fact that she held the highest rank on the ship and had been marginalized by the rag tag group of rebels had not set well with her. She listened as Gillis responded.

"I will take a group of fifty with me to the Virginia," Gillis volunteered. "I would like to have Francois and a squad of his platoon, Sophia, Wolvie, Nappy, Phoenix, Jack, Rolf, Porter, Choi, Giola and Lucius on my team. That would give us enough pilots, engine room operatives and weapons personnel to handle whatever is waiting for us. Since the Wisconsin is a science cruiser, I would appreciate a few doctorate level crew members to volunteer. Some of the Ortiz sisters are here with me and they are indicating that they would also like to come with us. We will use the Admiral One to transport us over. Once there, I will assume command as Captain of the Virginia while Giles will remain in command of the Wisconsin. Any questions?"

"I have one," Reed spoke up. "Most of my fellow science officers were on Cy-5 and are missing. I only saw three of my closest confidants left alive. That makes four of us. What kind of scientists do you want to take over with you?"

Gillis recognized that he was being tested. He smiled at Sophia before responding. "My preference would be an expert in radioactive research, or an astrophysicist or a doctorate in computer technology. My fear is that the crew of the Virginia abandoned ship to avoid some form of undetected leak or outer radiation risk. We will need additional assistance on the computer to secure the security tapes, provided they were not professionally removed. Do you have anyone that fits that description?"

Reed nodded, "Yes sir. I will send you two highly qualified individuals that can handle those tasks."

"Thank you," Gillis responded.

CHAPTER TWELVE

During the battle, Lila Zapata was able to make her way to the Engine Room without incident. She was greeted by three women in long sleeved, one piece orange uniforms. Each wore black boots and had thick black belts around their waists that held several engineering tools. The tallest woman smiled at Lila as she walked into the vast chamber of metal and machinery. She was standing on the third balcony transparent metal walkway with a magnetizer in one hand and a hand held communication device in the other.

"Hello down there. I am Lieutenant Maria Koh. Who are you?"

"I'm Lila Zapata. I'm a cadet from Clovis Academy. I was sent here to offer assistance on the dark matter converters. How are the repairs coming along?"

The three women exchanged glances. One of the women smiled at her and waived at her to indicate she should join them on the third balcony. "Glad you could join us. I am Lieutenant Sarah Abedini. I graduated from Clovis over five years ago. We are all that is left of the Engine crew. Most went to the space station which we just watched explode. Several others went AWOL after the Admiral and Captain left the ship. Several crew members stole some Raumschiffs and got away. Some others were blown up by those idiot pilots from Robert Andrews. We stayed and continued working on the repairs while all the excitement was going on around us."

Lila climbed up the ladders to the third level as Abedini spoke. When she reached the three women and shook their hands. The third introduced herself as Lieutenant Tara Woo.

"We completed the repairs on the dark matter converters," Koh told Lila. "It wasn't an easy task."

"They were damaged by an inside job," Woo said.

Lila looked above her and inspected the five grey and white cylinders that were connected to the black metal ceiling by large red and green cables and metallic tubes. The cylinders were each forty feet wide and thirty feet long. Lila noted that each of the cylinders had laser burns that made it clear someone or perhaps several individuals had sabotaged the cylinders. Without the dark matter convert, the *Wisconsin* would not be capable of sustaining the normal deep space travel speeds of over six hundred thousand kilometers an minute. The solar and nuclear power would be drained and the ship would have been forced to travel at a far lesser rate of speed.

"Any ideas who did it?" Lila asked the million dollar question.

Koh shrugged, "Climb inside the tubes and see for yourself. My best guess is that it had to be a coordination of a person with special knowledge of the converters and, at the same time, a person that had a great understanding of weaponry and metallurgy."

"Because a breach in the wrong portion of the cylinder would have caused massive explosions," Lila finished the thought for her.

"Correct," Woo smiled. "We should get you a uniform so you can be a part of our team. The perpetrator was like a skilled surgeon. He or she knew exactly where to cut, the amount of laser intensity that could be used without causing a fatal explosion, but would cripple the ship at the same time."

Lila nodded, "So it was an inside job. Whoever did this was a part of the crew. They were not on a suicide mission so they had to be cautious. What about the security tapes? Has anyone accessed those?"

"Not that we know of," Abedini reported. "The three of us suspect that there was more than one person involved and one of them had access to the security recordings. Admiral Gannon was really pissed when this happened. He ordered Lieutenant Winters to conduct a full investigation."

"Let me guess, no one was ever arrested?" Lila concluded.

"That's right," Koh affirmed. "Winters never located the perps. We always assumed that the security tapes had been erased by one of the perps involved."

"Well, I have no respect for Winters," Lila old them as she leaped upwards and took hold of the ladder handles on the side of one of the cylinders. She pulled herself upwards and opened the hatch on the bottom so that she could climb inside and inspect the repairs further.

"So you met him?" Woo asked.

"Yes, he was a real ass."

"What are you looking for?" Koh asked her.

"My husband is the one flying the Wisconsin," Lila told them. "He asked me to check out the repairs so he could make better judgment calls on how to maneuver the ship."

"You have a husband?" Abedini asked.

"Yes."

"You are really lucky," Abedini told her. "There are eight women to every man on this ship. All of the men are a bunch of misogynist pigs. Especially Winters. He has a wife or two on his home world but leaves them behind and tries to sleep with as many of us as he wants on the long, deep space voyages. A real jerk."

Lila nodded as she placed her foot on the ladder step and pulled out a small flashlight from her breast pocket. She shined it on the repair work and concentrated on the laser burns. She thought about Winters and his Spetsnaz beret that he wore with such pride. She recalled that Yuri Gorski had been a Spetsnaz graduate. Gorski had once told the gang at the Academy that part of the Spetsnaz training was to learn to use only enough force necessary to complete the mission. They were taught to avoid the overkill method of attack. Lila looked over the laser burns and concluded that Winters, the man assigned to discover the culprit may well have been the one that committed the act. The question was: Why? What would Winters have to gain by sabotaging his own science cruiser?

"Lila? Are you thinking what the three of us are thinking?" Koh called up to her.

"What are you thinking?" Lila asked.

"We concluded that Winters did this," Koh told her. "We reported our conclusions to Engineering Commander Smart. We never found out if he forwarded our fear to the Admiral. I guess that they are all dead now, so it is academic."

Lila pursed her lips and turned off her flashlight, "The Admiral is dead, yes. So is your Captain. But Commander Smart escaped the space station on one of the transport ships. I don't know what happened to Winters."

Lila waited a second for a response. Instead of continued conversation, Lila heard blood curdling screams of terror. She heard Koh begging for her life and more screams. Lila heard several clanging noises and then a third scream. Lila let go of the ladder handles and jumped down onto the walkway below her. She looked around at the sight around her and began to tremble with apprehension.

The bodies of Lieutenants Koh, Abedini and Woo were sprawled out on the metal walkway. Koh and Woo had their throats slashed. Abedini had two stab wounds in her chest. Their blood was still spilling onto the transparent metal walkway. Lila started to scream but Commander Smart covered her mouth with his hand and held her left arm behind her back.

"Shhhhhhh," Smart whispered into her ear. "Don't

scream. Everything will be fine if you cooperated with us. I am going to remove my hand so we can explain to you what happened. Nod if you agree not to scream."

Lila's heart was pounding in her chest like a bass drum beat. She gazed into Winters' eyes and looked down at the blood dripping knife in his hands. He obviously had killed the three engineering officers. Lila decided to play along and nodded.

Smart released her and she stood in silence, breathing heavily as Winters stepped over the three corpses and pointed down at them with the knife. "They didn't understand why we did what we had to do. We decided that they had to be silenced. But you have proven to be savvier than them. I was really impressed by some of the thigs that you and your friends did on Cy-5. You are like us, you are a survivor. Will you hear us out?"

"Yes," Lila responded softly. She had no choice. Smart was behind her and Winters in front. The fall from the railing would be three dozen feet which would almost certainly cause her some physical distress. That fact eliminated her attempting to escape by jumping over the protective rails.

"Good," Winters smiled at her. "You see, when the Civil War started, Jason and I were contacted by another party that felt that they could profit from the inevitable disaster. We were both paid very well to disable the dark matter energy converter to get the Wisconsin out of commission. Now, that these three nice officers repaired the damage, the Wisconsin can resume normal flight speeds. Our benefactor has lots of money and can pay any fee you desire for your silence. Koh was too idealistic to take the money. Abedini and Woo, well, they were collateral damage. The question is what is your price to keep silent?"

Lila swallowed hard. In the short moments she had interacted with Koh, she found her to be a kind person. The three deceased women did not deserve to die so young and so terribly. Lila wished she had turned on her communication device so that the conversation could be recorded for Jurgen, Les and Sophia to hear. She was alone and was cognizant that the next few words from her lips would determine whether she live or die.

"Who is your benefactor?" Lila managed to ask with a quivering voice.

"We are not willing to release that information as of yet," Smart responded. "That can be revealed after we have hush\ money transferred to an account in your name for your future use. Be wise, young lady. The people we work for are very powerful and will be in power once the Royals are removed. You can be given riches and a position in the new government to meet your needs. Your husband will be in position for his own command if you work with us."

Lila shook her head, "Jurgen would never go along with such an arrangement. He would only take a promotion that he felt that he deserved. If I cooperate with you, Jurgen will not."

Winters smiled maliciously, "Then I will gladly cut his throat like I did to Koh and Woo."

The threat against the life of her husband did not go over well. Lila kicked the knife out of Winters' hand. She whirled around and hit Smart in the face with a closed fist. Smart stumbled backwards as Lila ran past him. She didn't get far. Winters grabbed her long dark hair and yanked her backwards. The force of Winter's pull caused her to fall on her back with significant force. Lila felt herself lifted into the air by her hair. She was facing Winters, kicking and screaming at him. Winters smiled and showed her the bloody knife in his right hand.

"You should have cooperated," Winters whispered.

Lila screamed as Winters plunged the knife into her chest. He turned the blade upward, severing internal organs and blood vessels. Lila stopped kicking as she felt her life blood spilling out onto her tunic and dripping onto the metal floor. Her last sight was the sneering face of Winters as she took her last desperate breath. Her body went limp. Winters dropped Lila's corpse onto the metal floor and pulled the knife free.

"Shit," Smart whispered. "Now we will have Doernitz and Gillis as enemies."

Winters laughed, "They'll never know it was us. We will stage it to look like the four women fought and killed each other. They will do a crime scene investigation and find our fingerprints. Since you were chief of engineering you will be exonerated on that evidence. Me, I am wearing fake fingertips so they will never know that I was here. Let Gillis and his wife waste their time trying to determine how their friend died. We will never be discovered."

Smart shook his head. "We shouldn't have killed any of them, save Koh. We should have killed her in her quarters, away from the others. All of the other collateral damage is just going to open all this up to extra scrutiny."

Winters shrugged, "So what? Four dead bitches? Doernitz will find another hot looking piece of ass and forget her. These other three weren't married. Koh was a known cheap slut. I fucked her a few times. She was fun.

But no one will really miss them. You worry too much, Jason."

Smart shook his head at Winters in a disapproving manner. He regretted that he had ever entered into an alliance with the sadistic man in the first place.

"Now I am going to my quarters to shower and get rid of these clothes I am wearing. Give me ten minutes, the alert Major Docker that you found these four sluts knifed to death. By the time she gets an investigation going, I will be all cleaned up."

"We need to agree right her and now. No more killing. Okay?" Smart made the demand and met Winters' icy gaze.

There was an uncomfortable silence between them until Winters finally responded. "Don't worry. I am not going to kill anyone else. We just tied up any loose ends with these four. Besides, Docker will probably ask me to investigate this. Ha. Just like Gannon. Besides. I have a new hot girl that I am romancing. I don't need any more scandals around me if I am going to bed her."

"You a referring to that Ortiz traitor?" Smart asked him.

"Damn right," Winters smiled as he began climbing down the ladders. "She has a great body and I am going to lick her all over and ram my erection into every opening in her body. Come on, Jason. There are a ton of women on the ship now that suffered loss on Cy-5. They need to be consoled and have a shoulder to cry on. Use that and you can get all the ass in this ship."

Smart shook his head, "I'll think about it."

"Relax, Jason. It is a new world. The revolution is in full swing and you and I are wealthier than we ever dreamed. Smile. Enjoy life. Find some women and take what you want from them. Remember that integrity and morals will only get you killed in this universe. Take what you can when you can."

Smart looked over the four corpses and allowed Winters to exit the engine room. Smart knelt over the corpse of Woo. She had been a promising member of his engine room team. Smart closed his eyes and waited for several minutes to pass before he did as Winters requested. Smart dreaded what the reaction would be by others on the ship, especially DuBravac, Gillis and Doernitz.

Smart listened to the overhead communication chatter from Level One. He heard of the plans to board the *Virginia* and get her operational. He felt his side and determined that he needed medical attention for his ribs. He left the engine room and the four corpses behind. The further away from the crime scene the better. He was amazed that so many had been able to escape the metal death trap of Cy-5. If the Gods were kind, they would be able to sit out the remainder of the insurrection against the Royal Family in peace.

TO BE CONTINUED